He stared up at them as they reached his table, and they all sat down with him without speaking.

"Gents," he said, "can I help you?"

"We just thought we'd come over and join you," Bat said.

"You looked lonely," Short said.

"I assure you I'm not," the man said. "But I am always willing to meet new people. You are . . . ?"

"We've never met before?" Clint asked.

"I think I'd remember three such gentlemen as you," the man said.

"I don't remember you at all," Clint said, "but you do look . . . familiar to me."

Now the man shifted uncomfortably.

"It's as if . . . I knew someone who looked like you."

The seated man now struggled to keep from revealing anything with his face or his demeanor.

"It'll come to me, though," Clint said.

"If we stay long enough," Bat said.

"Oh, right. If we stay long enough."

"Well, I have to thank you gents," the man said. "You've made my breakfast very interesting."

"We have one more day," Clint replied. "to try to make your life interesting, as well."

The three of them walked away, never quite turning their backs on the other man.

H. L. J.

THE GUNSMITH

230

PAY DIRT

J. R. ROBERTS

J

JOVE BOOKS, NEW YORK

PAY DIRT

A Jove Book / published by arrangement with
the author

PRINTING HISTORY
Jove edition / February 2001

ONE

As far as Clint Adams was concerned he only had two faults. One was his curiosity, and the other was his loyalty to his friends.

Of course, some would say that the second one was not a fault, but the truth of the matter was it always got him into trouble. Still, he was too old to change his ways now.

What had brought him to Bended Knee, Arkansas, was a deposit into his bank account in Labyrinth, Texas, for a thousand dollars, which he knew nothing about.

"You mean somebody put a thousand dollars into your account without you knowing it?" his friend Rick Hartman asked.

"That's right."

"Why would somebody do that?"

"That's exactly what I want to know."

"How do you intend to find out?"

"I'm going to wait."

1

"For what?"

"For the person to reveal himself."

"What makes you think they will?"

"Think about it, Rick," Clint said. "Whoever put the money in there did it for a reason. Sooner or later, they'll let me know what it is."

Well, that hadn't exactly been the case. He did receive a telegram referring to the deposit, but all the message told him was that to find out what the money was for, and to be able to keep it, he had to go to a town he'd never heard of, in Arkansas, called Bended Knee.

"That's all it says?"

Clint handed the telegram across the table to Rick so he could read it himself.

"And you're gonna go?" Rick asked, handing it back.

"I think so."

"Why?" Rick asked. "You don't need the money."

"Everybody needs money," Clint said, "but you're right, I don't need this particular thousand dollars."

"Then why go?"

"Curiosity."

"What if it's a trap?"

"I guess I'll find that out, too."

"Does it ever occur to you to play it safe?" Rick asked.

Clint smiled and said, "Less and less the older I get."

So he had saddled Eclipse, his amazing Darley Arabian stallion, and ridden from Labyrinth, Texas, to Bended

Knee, Arkansas, which, to his educated eye, was a small town that didn't look to have much interest in growing. None of the buildings were less than ten or fifteen years old, and many were in need of repairs. How could someone from this town have a thousand dollars to waste just to get him here?

He rode down the main street, walking his horse slowly, staying alert, watching the rooftops and windows for a trap, but everything seemed to be fine—a quiet, peaceful town.

He found his way to the livery stable and dismounted. A man came out, wiping his hands on the seat of his britches, and asked, "Can I help ya?"

"I'd like to put my horse up."

"For how long?"

"I don't know, exactly," Clint said. "At least overnight."

The man was sixty, maybe a few years more, and he was chewing a huge wad of tobacco. He spat a brown stream off to one side and Clint could see by looking around that it wasn't the first.

"You here for the money?"

That surprised Clint.

"What money?"

The man backed off.

"Maybe you ain't here about the money," he said.

"What money are you talking about?"

"Ain't gonna say," the man said, turning reticent. "Maybe you is and maybe you ain't here for it. I guess you'll find out. I'll take your horse, though. Fine lookin' animal. I'll take good care of him for ya."

"I'd appreciate it," Clint said. "When I find out

what's going on I'll let you know how long I'm staying."

"Suits me," the man said. He peered at Clint, then
spat another brown stream before saying, "You ain't
the onliest one, ya know."

"The only one for what?"

"What come fer the money."

"Look," Clint said, "either tell me what you're talking about or just forget all about—"

"Ain't gonna say," the man said, turning to go into
the stable with Eclipse. "Ain't my place. You'll find
out soon enough—you and the others."

"What others?" Clint asked, but the man had gone
inside.

TWO

Clint walked back the way he had come on horseback, heading for the hotel he had spotted during the ride in. As he entered the lobby he wasn't surprised to find it badly furnished, with a worn sofa missing a leg and listing to one side. The clerk, too, seemed to be listing to one side as he stood behind the desk, but while the sofa leaned to the right, the clerk was leaning to the left.

"Help ya?" the man asked.

"I need a room."

"Got plenty," the clerk said. "Jest sign the register."

He looked to be in his late fifties, and Clint could have sworn that he and the liveryman were brothers. All that was missing was the huge plug of tobacco in his cheek.

Clint accepted the register book and wrote his name in. There was a space for where he was from, but he left that blank.

When he was finished the man turned the book around and read the name. He looked up at Clint in surprise, and then squinted with one eye—the left one, which was the side he was listing to.

"You here fer the money?"

"What money?"

The man straightened and said, "Maybe you ain't."

Maybe he was and maybe he wasn't, but he sure was getting tired of being asked.

"You wouldn't happen to be related to the man at the livery, would you?" Clint asked.

"He's my brother," the man replied.

"I thought so."

"He bother you?"

"No more or less than you are," Clint said. "Can I have my key?"

"Sure thing." The clerk turned, took a key from a board behind him and handed it to Clint.

"Number ten. Overlooks the street."

"Fine."

Clint picked up his saddlebags and rifle, carried them to the stairs and walked up, aware that the man was still watching him. He figured he could have forced either man to tell him what they were talking about, but he knew he'd find out sooner or later. He was curious, however, about what the liveryman had said about him not being the only one.

What was that about?

He was satisfied with the location of the room. It did overlook the street, but there was no outside access to his window. The bed was rickety, but he thought it would hold him. There was a chest of drawers that looked so fragile he doubted he'd use it. At least there was a pitcher of water and a basin to wash in. He used it to clean some of the trail dust from his face.

The room smelled musty so he opened the window to air it out. He stood there staring down at the street, drying his hands and face, and at that moment a rider came into view. The man's face was not visible from this angle, hidden by the brim of his hat, but the way he sat atop his horse was very familiar. He watched until the rider was out of sight. He decided to go downstairs and wait for the man in front of the hotel since, as far as he could see, this would be the only place for the man to stay.

"Is the room all right fer ya?" the clerk asked as Clint reached the lobby again.

"It's fine," he said, and headed for the door. Right outside he found a wooden chair that was stronger than anything he had seen in the lobby, or in his room. He put the chair right up against the building, then settled into it to await the arrival of the rider.

As the man came walking up the street from the livery Clint could see that he was right. The clothing he was wearing was not of the usual quality, but then he looked to have ridden a long way. He was carrying saddlebags and a rifle and while his head was tilted down so that his face was still hidden from view by the brim of his hat, Clint easily recognized the walk.

The man reached the hotel, lifted his head, looked at Clint and smiled broadly.

"A thousand dollars?" his good friend Bat Masterson asked.

Clint nodded.

"In the bank," he said.

"With no hint what it's for."

"Or how it got there."

"Curiosity is going to get us killed one of these days," Bat said.

"Probably."

"Anybody else here?"

"Not yet," Clint said, "but I'm starting to get a bad feeling."

"I'll just go inside, get a room, stow my gear and we'll go and get a drink and see what we can figure out."

"I'll wait here."

Bat stared at Clint, then said, "Damn, it's good to see you."

"Same to you, Bat."

Bat went inside and Clint settled back into the chair to wait.

THREE

Bended Knee was small enough for Clint and Bat to walk up and down both sides of the street and see the entire town. It had one saloon, and they stopped in it to have a beer and talk. As they entered, they caught the attention of everyone in the place—the bartender and one other man seated at a table, contemplating a glass of whiskey.

"Two beers," Clint said to the bartender.

"Comin' up," the man said.

He drew the two beers and set them on the counter, then leaned his elbows on the bar.

"You fellas here for the money?"

Clint and Bat looked at each other, and then Bat asked, "What money?"

The bartender stood up straight.

"Never mind," he muttered. "Maybe you ain't."

Clint and Bat took their beers to a table in a corner so that they could each sit with their back to a wall.

"Did the liveryman ask you that?" Clint asked.

"Yeah," Bat said, "and the desk clerk at the hotel.

9

You think they're talking about the thousand dollars?"

"I don't know," Clint said, "but the next person who asks me that is going to have to explain themselves."

"Nobody's contacted you yet?" Bat asked.

"I only got here a half an hour before you did."

"Coming from where?"

"Texas."

"I was in Denver," Bat said.

"You suppose anybody else got a deposit in their bank account like we did?"

"Why should we be the only ones?"

"And who would you think those others would be?"

"Beats me," Bat said. "But I'll bet as soon as they arrive we'll be able to figure out what this is all about."

"Doesn't feel like a trap," Clint said.

"Maybe not," Bat said, "but it's too quiet. And where would somebody from this town get the money to send us each a thousand dollars?"

"And who knows how many more?"

"Like I said," Bat commented, "curiosity's gonna get us killed one of these days, but damn it, nobody just gives away a thousand dollars."

"You've got that right," Clint said. "This whole thing must have something to do with money, though."

"Otherwise why does everyone in this town seem to know something about money?"

Clint was staring at the bartender.

"He look familiar to you?"

The man was in his forties, with an angular face and thinning hair.

"He sort of looks like the clerk at the hotel," Bat said.

"And the liveryman," Clint said. "And those other two are brothers."

"Another brother?" Bat asked.

"Odd."

"Maybe they should have called this town 'Three Brothers'," Bat suggested.

"If that's all there are."

"You think maybe they're behind this?"

"A liveryman, a hotel clerk and a bartender?" Clint asked. "I wouldn't think so."

"Don't be a snob, Clint."

"When have I ever been a snob?"

"Well, don't start now," Bat said. "Among the three of them they probably have three of the better businesses in town."

"Enough to send out . . . how many thousands of dollars? And for what purpose?"

Bat sipped his beer and said, "I guess that's what we're going to be sitting around here waiting to find out."

Little by little the saloon began to get busier. Eventually, to while away the time, Clint and Bat were able to convince three other men to join them in a game of poker, for low stakes.

They played for a few hours, Clint and Bat the only ones winning, and splitting the profits fairly evenly. During the course of the evening they kept expecting someone to approach them and offer an explanation for why they had been sent the money and invited to Bended Knee, but it didn't happen. One by one the three men they were playing cards with tapped out, until they were the only two left.

"High card for the whole poke?" Bat asked.

"Why not?" Clint asked.

They pushed all of the money they had each won into the center of the table, along with the money they had each started with. Bat shuffled and placed the deck on the table.

"You first," Bat said.

Clint drew a card, held it so only he could see it, then Bat drew his and held it close to his chest. At the same time they dropped their cards on the table. Clint had a King of Spades, and Bat had a King of Clubs.

"That's the way the night has been going," Bat said. "Split the pot again."

They both looked at the money on the table, which totaled about sixty dollars. They had been playing for *very* low stakes, indeed.

"Want to play higher stakes?" Bat asked.

"Head to head?"

Bat nodded.

"How much did you have in mind?" Clint asked.

"Well," Bat said, "we each have an extra thousand in our bank account."

Clint thought a moment, then asked, "Who deals?"

FOUR

They used the same money that was on the table, but increased the value of each coin and bill. They passed the money back and forth across the table for a while, but neither of them was able to get any further ahead so, once again, they quit even.

Bat collected the cards and set them aside, and they both surveyed the room. For a small town there seemed to be a lot of men in the saloon. No women, though. Perhaps the owner couldn't afford to hire saloon girls, or maybe there were just no women in town willing to take the job.

"I've had it," Clint said. "I'm going to turn in. Maybe tomorrow will bring an explanation."

"And if it doesn't?" Bat asked. "How many more days are you willing to give it?"

"If someone doesn't talk to us tomorrow," Clint said, standing up, "or if somebody else we know doesn't come riding in, I'm leaving the day after tomorrow."

Bat stood and said, "Sounds fair to me."

Together they left the saloon. They'd started walking

13

toward the hotel when Bat reached out and lightly touched Clint's arm.

"I hear them," Clint said.

"Behind us."

"Yes," Clint said.

"Let's cross the street," Bat suggested.

Together they stepped off the boardwalk and started to cross, but the men stalking them were not pros. As soon as Clint and Bat were in the middle of the street the three drew their guns. As they cocked the hammers of their revolvers both Clint and Bat whirled, dropped, and drew their guns. They each fired, the muzzle flashes lighting the night, and then it was quiet again except for the sound of men groaning in pain.

Bat and Clint rushed the three fallen men and kicked away the guns, which had fallen to the dirt. Quickly they checked and found one dead, two wounded.

"Well, at least the one I shot is dead," Bat said.

Clint was about to argue with his friend when he decided against it.

"Fine," he said, "you killed one, and I shot and wounded two."

Bat frowned when he realized he was not coming out ahead on this.

"Now wait a minute—"

"I'm agreeing with you," Clint said, dragging one man over into the moonlight so he could see his face. "Ha!"

"What?"

"Just as I thought," Clint said. "Our three poker buddies."

Bat rolled the dead man over and studied his face in

the darkness, Sure enough, he recognized him. He turned to the third man and nudged him with his foot, making sure the toe of his boot brushed against his wounded shoulder.

"Oh!" the man cried out.

"Who sent you?" Bat asked.

"Nobody—ow!"

Bat nudged him harder and asked, "Who sent you?"

"Nobody," the man shouted.

"Then why'd you try to kill us?"

"You took the last of our money," the man said. "We wanted to get it back."

"The last of your money?" Bat asked. "What? Fifty, sixty dollars?"

"Twenty was mine," the man said. "I lost the most."

"So it was your idea to kill us and take it back?" Clint asked.

"Yeah—no, I mean, no, my idea—"

This time Bat kicked him and the man passed out.

"Sonofabitch wanted to kill us for twenty dollars!" he snapped.

"I wonder if this town has a lawman?" Clint asked, looking around.

"If they do he's a heavy sleeper."

"Looks like everyone is," Clint said. "Nobody even came out of the saloon to see what was going on."

"So what do you want to do with them?" Bat asked.

"You three live in town?" Clint asked the wounded man he was still holding onto.

"N-no, sir. We're just passin' through."

"Take your dead friend, then, and keep passing," Clint said.

"B-but me and . . . and Joe, we need a doctor."

"Get one in the next town," Bat said. "If we see you here tomorrow we'll kill you. Understand?"

Clint shook the man so that he answered, "Y-yes, I understand."

"Good," Bat said, "make sure your friend understands, too."

Clint leaned over so that his face was only an inch from the other man's.

"Backshooters are the worst vermin in the world," he said. "I'd kill you and your friend but then we'd have to clean up the mess. So now you and your friend can clean it up."

"What about Hiram?" the man asked, indicating the dead man.

"That's the mess," Clint said, straightening. "Clean it up."

He and Bat backed away from the fallen men, still holding their guns, and then turned and melted away into the darkness, holstering their weapons.

They stopped in front of the hotel to eject their spent shells and replace them before holstering their guns again. They had made it this far without running into any curious onlookers.

"Weird town," Bat said.

"Odd," Clint agreed.

"If there's a lawman we might have to talk to him tomorrow."

Clint shrugged and said, "Let him come to us. If he does, we'll tell him what happened."

They took one last look up and down the dark street, then turned and went inside.

FIVE

Clint woke early the next morning, poured some water in the basin and washed the sleep out of his eyes. He wasn't fooling himself. Today he and Bat would have to talk to someone about what had happened last night. You don't just kill a man and walk away.

He looked out the window and realized that he could see the area in the street where the shooting had taken place. Squinting his eyes, though, he could not make out any blood in the street, and there should have been some there—unless someone had cleaned it up.

He strapped on his gun, left his room and went down to the lobby.

"Mornin'," the desk clerk said—the same man who had checked him—and Bat—in the day before.

"Where can a man get some breakfast?" Clint asked.

"Go out the door, turn right, go about three blocks and then turn right again. There'll be a café there, just off the corner."

"What's the name of it?"

"Ain't got a name," the man said, "but you can't

17

miss it. You'll be able to smell it a block away."

Clint turned to leave, then turned back to the man.

"I saw a bartender in the saloon last night who looked a lot like you," he said.

"That'd be my brother Caleb."

"How many brothers do you have?"

"Well, there's Caleb—he's the baby—then Harley—you met him, he runs the livery, then there's me . . . just the three of us, I guess."

"And Caleb owns the saloon?"

"That's right."

"And you own this hotel?"

"Right again."

"And there's no other brothers?"

"Not a one," the man said, rubbing his jaw, "unless Maw snuck one in on us."

"So I'm not going to run into anyone else who looks like you and your brothers?"

"I didn't say that," the man said. "Got a passel of cousins out there and, oh, yeah, if'n you eat at the café you'll meet our two sisters."

Clint studied the man's angular features and his bony physique, and shuddered to think what the sisters must look like.

He followed the desk clerk's directions and, sure enough, about a block away he was able to smell the food. He found the café a couple of doors off the corner. It was a plain storefront with big, bare windows, and inside he could see tables and chairs. Most of them were empty, but there were a few that were taken, two couples sitting together and another with two men eat-ing together. As he entered, a woman came out of what must have been the kitchen, spotted him and walked toward him. She must have been a waitress hired by the desk clerk's sisters. She had long blonde hair, clear, smooth skin and was wearing a simple cotton dress that molded itself to a lush body. As she approached him he could see her breasts moving beneath the dress, almost like the ripples in a lake after you've tossed a stone into it.

She smiled broadly, revealing fine, healthy white teeth. There were no lines at the corner of her eyes or her mouth, and he judged her to be about twenty-six or -seven.

"Can I help you?" she asked.

"I'd like some breakfast."

"You're new in town, ain'tcha?" she asked, her hands on her hips. Her back was ramrod straight, and her generous breasts were thrust out at him. Her posture was definitely flirtatious.

"Just rode in yesterday."

"Well, come on, then," she said. "You'll be lookin' for a good meal, and you came to the right place."

"The desk clerk at the hotel told me to come here," Clint said, following her to a table.

"That'd be my brother Adam."

"Your . . . brother?"

She turned to face him.

"That's right."

"And . . . Harley, and Caleb, they're also your brothers?"

"That's right."

Clint decided that this must be the sister who got all

the looks. The other sister was probably still in the kitchen and . . . at that moment another blonde woman, a little older, but no less stunning in face or form, came out of the kitchen carrying a tray of food.

"That's my older sister, Kate," she said. "I'm Kitty."

He stared at Kate as she bent over to lay down the plates of food she was carrying. She was dressed the same way, a cotton dress that clung to her. He could see that she was even a little more full-bodied than Kitty was, and he marveled at how these two women could be related to the rail-thin, angular faced men he'd already met.

"Ain't she pretty?" Kitty asked. "Kate got all the looks in our family."

"Kate got—"

She pushed him so that he sat down in a chair and she said, "I'll bring you some coffee while you decide what you wanna eat."

He watched as she and her sister disappeared into the kitchen again, and then sat there frowning, trying to put these two sisters together with their three brothers, simply not being able to do it.

SIX

Clint was just starting on his breakfast when Bat Masterson walked in. Bat saw Clint and joined him before either Kate or Kitty could come out and seat him.

"You, too?" Bat asked.

"Seems like the only place in town to eat."

Bat sat down and lowered his voice.

"The desk clerk told me his sisters run this place," he said. "Can you imagine what they must look like?"

"I don't have to imagine," Clint said.

"Oh, that's right," Bat said, sitting back, "you've got your breakfast, so you've seen them—and you still have your appetite?"

"Just barely."

"God help us," Bat said, and then Kitty came out of the kitchen. Clint waved her over.

"Oh, you have a friend with you," she said.

"That's right," Clint said. "Your brother sent him over here, too."

"He likes to send his guests over here," she said. "We give them a small discount." She looked at Bat, who was staring at her, open-mouthed. "What can I get for you, sir?"

Bat stared a few moments longer before stirring.

"I'll, uh, have what he's having."

"Steak and eggs, coming up." She retrieved a coffee cup from another table and put it in front of him, then returned to the kitchen.

"You sonofabitch," Bat said, as Clint poured him a cup of coffee.

"Wait until you see the other one."

"Is she . . . ?"

"More of the same."

Bat frowned and asked, "How is that possible? How can they be related to those three . . ."

"I know," Clint said. "Obviously, they must take after their mother."

"What must their father have looked like?"

"Who knows?" Clint asked. "It could be a combination of genes that produced them, you know."

At that moment Kate came out, served a table and returned to the kitchen.

"That was the other one?"

"Uh-huh."

"I can see what you mean by more of the same."

"She's the older one," Clint said. "According to Kitty, Kate's the one with the looks."

"Jesus," Bat said, "the younger doesn't *know* how fantastic she looks?"

"I guess not."

"How is *that* possible?"

"Maybe there was a different standard of beauty in their house," Clint suggested.

"My God," Bat said, "by any standard they're both—"

"I know."

"This could make the stay in Bended Knee a little more interesting," Bat said.

"I was thinking that, too," Clint admitted, "but we can't forget why we're here, or what happened last night."

"We don't know why we're here, so how can we forget it?" Bat asked. "As for what happened last night, I still haven't seen a lawman in this town, have you?"

"No," Clint said, "but—"

He stopped short when Kitty appeared with Bat's breakfast.

"Kitty," Clint said, "can I ask you something?"

"Go ahead."

"Is there a sheriff, or a marshal in this town?"

"Why?" she asked. "Is there something wrong with the food? Are you gonna have us arrested?"

"There's nothing wrong with the food," Clint said. "It's wonderful. We were just . . . wondering."

"Well, yeah, we got a sheriff," Kitty said. "He ain't so much of a sheriff, but we got one."

"It doesn't sound like you have a very high opinion of him."

"Well," she said, "I know him pretty well."

"Oh," Clint said, "boyfriend?"

"No," she said, with a definite shake of her head.

"Not another brother?" Bat asked.

"No," she said, "we only have three of those."

"Wait," Clint said, "let me guess. Cousin?"

"That's it," she said. "He's our cousin."

"How'd you know that?" Bat asked.

"There are a whole passel of cousins out here," Clint told Bat.

"You been talking to my brother Adam again," Kitty said.

"That I have."

"Well, the sheriff's name is Rupert."

"And does he have the same family last name?"

"Oh, yeah," she said. "Me and Kate are the only girls, and we ain't married, so we all got the same family name."

"Which is?"

"Oh," she said, "sorry, I'm being rude. Our last name is Cahill."

"The Cahills of Bended Knee," Bat said.

"You've heard of us?" she asked.

"No," Clint said, "should we have?"

"Well," she said, "we do make a pretty mean steak and eggs."

With that she turned and went to wait on another table.

SEVEN

Bat and Clint finished their breakfasts while continuing to watch Kate and Kitty Cahill walk back and forth from the kitchen.

"Okay," Clint said, as they finished the second pot of coffee, "we've got to get out of here now."

"Why?" Bat asked. "What else is there to do?"

"Well," Clint said, "for one thing we can go and see the sheriff."

"What for?" Bat asked. "He's one of the Cahill men. You think they seem like they got a brain among them?"

"They own most of the businesses in town, it seems," Clint said, "and they've got the sheriff's office. You think they're really as dumb as they seem?"

"Probably not," Bat admitted, grudgingly. "But I know they're as ugly as they seem."

"Okay," Clint said, "you got me there."

"But not their women," Bat said, smiling as Kitty started toward them to see what else she could do for them.

25

•   •   •

After they left the café Bat reluctantly agreed to go and
see the sheriff with Clint.

"Those men are gone," he reasoned, "and they took
the dead one with them. There isn't even any blood in
the street."

"I know that," Clint said. "Look, why don't I go and
see him myself? I'll tell him the story, but I'll leave
you out of it."

"No," Bat said, with a pained expression. "You need
me to back up the story. Come on, we'll go and see
him together."

Clint put his hand on his friend's shoulder and said,
"Thanks."

"Besides," Bat added, "I'm dying to see what a Cahill cousin looks like."

They entered the sheriff's office and the man looked
up from his desk.

"He looks just like them," Bat whispered, "jug ears
and all."

"Help you fellers?"

"Are you Sheriff Cahill?" Clint asked.

"That's me."

"Kitty said we'd find you here."

"You ate at Kate's and Kitty's?"

"Breakfast," Clint said.

"Best food in town," the sheriff said. "What can I
do for you gents?"

"Allow us to introduce ourselves," Bat said. "My
name is Bat Masterson."

"And my name is Clint Adams."

The Cahill cousin stared at them for a few moments, and then said, "I'll be damned. You here for the money, ain't ya?"

"Well, it's a myth," Sheriff Cahill said. "You know what a myth is?"

"Yes," Bat said, "something that isn't true."

Clint and Bat were sitting across the desk from the sheriff, who was responding to their joint demand that he tell them what money everybody was talking about.

"See, there used to be a gang hereabouts," Rupert Cahill said, "and they was supposed to have robbed them lots of banks and trains and stages and such and buried the money hereabouts."

"What gang?" Bat asked.

"What was the name?" Clint asked.

"Well, now," the lawman said, "bein' an officer of the law and all I'm just a touch embarrassed to answer that."

"The Cahill Gang?" Bat asked.

"I'm afraid so," the sheriff said. "See my pappy, and Kitty's pappy, they was supposed to be the leaders of this gang."

"And they buried money around here?" Clint asked.

"That's the myth," Rupert Cahill said. "Lots of money."

"So why does everybody think we're here looking for the money?" Clint asked.

"Because," the sheriff said, spreading his hands, "why else would strangers come to Bended Knee?"

"Now there's something I've been wondering about," Bat said.

"What's that?" Cahill asked.

"The name of this town," Bat said. "How did it come to be called Bended Knee?"

"Well," Cahill said, "the way I hear it both my pappy and my uncle was constantly bein' begged by my ma and my aunt to give up the outlaw life and settle down."

"Here?" Clint asked.

"Well, there was no 'here' here at that time," Cahill said. "So my pappy and my uncle built this here town for my ma and my aunt."

"And they named it Bended Knee because . . . ?" Bat asked.

"Because my ma and my aunt used to get down on bended knee when they was beggin' them to quit."

Clint and Bat looked at each other, and then back at Sheriff Rupert Cahill, who was smiling real wide at them.

" 'Course," Cahill said, "that could be just another one of them myths."

EIGHT

After they talked about the money Clint and Bat told the sheriff about the poker game, and what happened after it. When they were done Rupert Cahill dug at something in his right ear with the tip of his little finger, his right eye closed as he did so. Bat and Clint waited until he was done.

"Don't see that there's anything I can do about that," the lawman finally said. "I ain't got a body, so I got nothin' says you killed a man—except your word, of course."

"So we can go?" Bat asked.

"You can leave my office," Cahill said, "or leave town, whichever one you mean. I ain't got no reason to hold you."

Bat stood up, but Clint remained seated.

"Come on, Clint," Bat said. "The sheriff said we can go."

Clint was studying Rupert Cahill, wondering if he should bring up the thousand dollars both he and Bat had found in their bank accounts.

29

"You mind me askin' a question?" Cahill asked, before Clint could make up his mind.

"Go ahead, Sheriff," Bat said. "You answered all ours. Guess we owe you the same courtesy."

"What brings two famous gents like yerselves to Bended Knee?" the lawman asked.

Before Clint could say a word Bat said, "We're just passing through, Sheriff."

"So you'll be on yer way tomorrow?"

"That's possible," Bat said. "I guess that depends on how we feel when we get up in the morning."

Abruptly, Clint stood up.

"Guess we better let you get to work," he said.

He'd decided not to say anything about the money.

"You gents enjoy the rest of yer stay now, ya here?" Cahill said as they walked to the door. "And don't you go killin' nobody else!"

"You were going to tell him, weren't you?" Bat said when they got outside.

"I thought about it."

"What stopped you?"

"I don't know," Clint said. "I guess I just don't think he'd know anything about it."

They started walking aimlessly, just something to do while they talked.

"You ever hear of the Cahill Gang?" Bat asked.

"Never."

"And what do you think about this buried money?"

"Probably like he says," Clint replied. "A myth."

"Still," Bat said, "if it was around here and somebody managed to find it and dig it up—"

"You looking to go prospecting, Bat?" Clint asked. "Or treasure-hunting, maybe?"

"I'm just saying it's interesting."

"Do you know what would happen if somebody came along and found that money?"

"They'd be rich."

"They'd be dead," Clint said.

"The Cahills?" Bat asked, after a moment.

"Why would they stick around here if they didn't believe the myth?" Clint asked.

"So they're waiting for somebody to find it so they can take it away from them."

"Probably."

"Why don't they just find it themselves?"

"They've probably tried," Clint said. "They've probably looked and looked and haven't been able to find it."

"You'd think if their fathers did bury the money they would have told at least one of the kids."

"Maybe they did."

"You mean one of them knows, and isn't telling the others?"

"Again," Clint said, "maybe."

"Not the way to treat your own family."

"What the hell," Clint said, "there probably isn't any money, anyway."

"So then," Bat said, "we're right back where we started. Who sent us that money and who wanted us here?"

They reached the end of town, crossed the street and started back the other way again.

"So what do we do while we're waiting . . . what? One more day?"

"One more," Clint said. "That's all I intend to give it."

"Poker again?"

"No," Clint said. "That got us into enough trouble."

"What then?"

"I think I'll just go and sit in front of the hotel," Clint said, "and see if anyone else rides into town to-day."

"That's it?" Bat asked. "Just sit?"

"That's it."

They walked along in silence for a little while and as they started to approach the hotel Bat said, "Well, maybe I'll sit with you—for a while, anyway."

"How long is a while?"

Bat smiled and said, "Maybe just until the lovely Cahill sisters close their café for the day."

NINE

"You like being part of a big family?" Clint asked Bat a little while later.

"Wha—" Bat had fallen asleep in his chair.

"You're part of a big family, right?"

"Not real big."

"But you've got brothers."

"Oh, sure."

"What was that like?"

"It was okay," Bat said. "I'll tell you, though, it really comes in handy when you need somebody to watch your back."

"I never had any family," Clint said. "No parents, no brothers or sisters I can remember. No cousins."

"You miss that?"

"I don't know if I miss it," Clint said. "I never had it."

"Do you think you'd like it?" Bat asked. "Are you wishing you had—"

"No," Clint said, "not wishing. I'm just thinking

about all these Cahills. Brothers, sisters, cousins—do you think they all like each other?"

"Probably not."

"But what if they all needed to gather 'round and pull together as a family?" Clint asked.

"Then I guess they'd do it."

"Because blood is thicker than water?"

"That's one reason."

"What would your reason be?"

"Me? I like my brothers, and I think they like me."

"No jealousy?"

"Nope."

"You wouldn't go against each other for money?"

"Nope."

"A lot of money?"

Bat turned his head to look at Clint.

"Would you go against me for money?"

"No."

"And you're not even my brother."

"You're my friend," Clint said. "That's worth more to me than any amount of money—and I know you feel the same way."

"You do?"

"Yes, I do."

"I wonder— Hey," Bat said.

"What?"

"Rider."

They both sat forward in their chairs and stared up the street.

"See him?" Clint asked.

"I hear him—or his horse."

Clint heard the horse too now. They watched for the

rider to come into view, and when he did they both knew him.

"I'll be damned," Bat said.

"Does this surprise you?"

"No," Bat said, "but I was hoping it would be somebody else."

"Why?"

"Because then it would have been easier to figure out where we all were when whatever happened happened."

As the rider came closer they both stood up and he spotted them. With a smile he directed his horse toward the hotel, where he reined in.

"What the hell are you two doin' here?" Luke Short asked.

Clint and Bat both looked up at their friend, and possibly the best poker player they had ever known.

"Same as you, probably," Bat said.

"A thousand dollars?" Short asked.

"That's right," Clint said.

Short looked around, then back at his friends.

"Do we know anything about it yet?"

"Not a thing," Bat said.

"Anybody else in town?"

"We're the only three, so far," Clint said.

"Well, that doesn't help," Short said.

"That's what Bat was just saying."

Short looked at the hotel.

"This the only place to stay?"

"Yep," Clint said.

"Livery?"

"End of the street," Bat said.

"A saloon, I hope."

"There is one," Clint said. "Get your horse taken care of, get yourself a room and we'll take you over there and buy you a drink."

"Better be a big drink," Luke Short said, "one that's worth ridin' all this way for."

"I thought that's what the thousand dollars was for?" Bat asked.

"I don't need a thousand dollars that bad," Short said, "but I'd sure as hell like to know who put it in my bank account, how and why."

"That's what we all want to know, Luke," Clint said.

"So far," Bat said, "whatever it is was worth three thousand dollars to . . . well, to whoever it is."

"When you talk like that," Short said, "you make my head spin. I'll be right back, boys. Don't go away, all right?"

"Where would we go?" Bat asked, spreading his arms. "This is the whole town."

"I'm getting unhappier by the minute," Short said, and rode toward the livery.

TEN

Clint and Bat remained in place until Short returned and checked into the hotel. Then they walked with him over to the café, because he complained of being hungry.

"Well," Clint said, "the one thing this town can offer you is good food."

"And something to look at while you eat," Bat said.

On the way they told Short about the Cahill family, and the Cahill family myth. Bat also took great pleasure in telling him about the Cahill sisters. When they got there it was Kitty who greeted them, and Short saw that they were right about the women.

"Back so soon?" she asked. "You must really like our food."

"It's our friend," Clint said. "He just got to town and he's hungry."

"He's older," Bat confided, "and if he doesn't eat regularly he gets real cranky."

Short scowled, but Kitty smiled at him and said,

"You don't look so old to me, but we'll feed you, anyway."

"Thank you," Short said.

"This way. Your table is still available."

She led them to the same table they had used that morning.

"Coffee for all three of us," Clint said, "but food for one."

"What will you have?" she asked Short.

He looked at Clint, who said, "The steak and eggs were delicious."

"Steak," Short said, "no eggs."

"Vegetables?"

"Please."

She looked at Clint and asked, "Did you go and see Rupert?"

"We did."

"What did you think."

"He's . . . an interesting man."

"Rupert?" she asked, then laughed and went off to get their coffee.

"Very pretty," Short said. "And the sister?"

"The same," Bat said, "only more so."

"So what else have you fellas found out aside from the fact that this family runs the town and has a myth?"

"Not much," Bat said. "We assumed there would be more people joining us, but we hoped it wouldn't be you."

"Thanks."

"I mean," Bat said, "that we three have been in the same place at the same time a lot. The three of us being summoned here doesn't really tell us anything."

"I see what you mean," Short said. "We need someone unusual to ride in, someone the three of us may
have played poker with once."

"Then maybe we can figure out what happened then
that would have us summoned here now," Clint said.

"And who," Bat said.

"So we all figure this the same way?" Short said.
"There's one person who wants us all here?"

"Yeah, but who?" Bat asked. "And what for?"

"Well," Short said, "a surprise, maybe, something
worth a thousand dollars a piece."

"A good surprise or a bad surprise?" Clint asked.

"Maybe a poker game," Bat said.

"Maybe," Short said, "revenge."

They stopped talking until Kitty poured them all coffee and then returned to the kitchen. They were the
only customers in the place.

"So if there's the possibility that somebody's setting
a trap," Short asked, "what the hell are we doing here?"

"Curiosity," Bat said.

"And ego," Clint added.

"What?" Bat asked. "How do you figure that?"

"Come on, Bat," Clint said, "we're all here because
we figure we can handle whatever comes along."

"He's got a point," Short said, sipping coffee.

"Well," Bat said, "I don't like that point. That sure
sounds like something that might get us killed one
day."

"Could be," Short said, "but I'd rather live this way
than the alternative. If there's someone here who's got
something to say to me . . . well, I want to hear it."

"So do I," Clint said.

"Well," Bat said, "I'm sure glad none of us were influenced by the money."

"A thousand dollars," Short said, "won't even get us into some of the better poker games in Portsmouth Square."

"I was in San Francisco just last month . . ." Bat started.

Kitty brought Luke Short his steak and vegetables and he and Bat and Clint talked about San Francisco and gambling and did not get back to the matter at hand until he had finished his lunch.

"We have some fresh pie," Kitty said, as she collected his plate.

"Peach?" Clint asked.

"Peach, apple and rhubarb."

"Peach for me," Clint said.

"Apple," Bat said.

"I'll try the rhubarb," Short said.

"And more coffee," Clint added.

"Comin' up, gents."

When she came out with the pie she was carrying two slices while Kate carried the other, and the next pot of coffee. Short's eyes popped as he saw what his friends had meant by Kate being the same as Kitty, "only more so." She was a full-bodied, solid woman.

"We could be waiting in worse places for a surprise," he said aloud.

Bat and Clint nodded their agreement.

ELEVEN

Rupert Cahill left his office, locking the door behind him, and walked across the street to the hotel. As he entered he looked around, but there was nobody in the lobby except for his cousin Adam.

"Anybody around?" he asked.

"No," Adam said. "They left with the new feller; just got in today."

"What's his name?"

"Luke Short."

"So we got Clint Adams, Bat Masterson and now Luke Short in town?" the sheriff asked.

"That's right."

"Where's Caleb?"

"Tending bar, I suspect."

"And Harley?"

"At the livery."

"Reckon I better go and talk to them."

"What for?"

" 'Cause I don't want them doin' nothin' stupid, that's why."

"Rupert," Adam Cahill said, "you let me worry about my brothers doin' somethin' stupid, you hear? They don't answer to you, they answer to me."

"I'm the one with the badge," Rupert said.

"You can lose that badge just as quick as you got it."

"Now, Adam," Rupert said, "you got no call—"

"And another thing."

"What?"

"Stop sniffin' around my sister Kitty."

"Hey, now—"

"It ain't right," Adam said. "She's yore cousin. It ain't natural."

"Well, now," Rupert said, "seems to me it were natural enough for my momma and pappy."

"Well, it ain't natural for my sister," Adam said. "Find yourself another woman."

"There ain't no other women in town," Adam said. "Jest Kitty and Kate."

"Don't even think about Kate," Adam said. "You get an itch you go and see Milly."

"Milly's a whore," Rupert complained. "And an ugly whore at that. It ain't right for a sheriff to go to a whore."

"Well, it ain't right for a sheriff to go to his cousin, neither," Adam said. "Now, I'm a-warnin' you, Rupert. Stay away from my sisters. You hear me?"

"I hear," Rupert said. "I'm gonna walk aroun' town."

"You walk aroun' town all you want," Adam said. "You jest stay away from those three until the time comes."

Adam turned and stormed back to the hotel desk.

"Adam, goddamnit, you're a-tellin' me I can't go near them, I can't go near yore sisters and I can't talk to your brothers. I can't go nowhere near none of my kin?"

"I just don't want no mistakes, Rupert."

"I ain't gonna make no mistakes, Adam."

"Let's just keep our heads, you hear?" Adams said. "We don't wanna be arguin' among ourselves."

"I ain't arguin'," Rupert said, calming down. "I'm jest sayin', is all."

"Well, okay then."

"Okay."

"See ya."

"I'll see ya later," Rupert said, and walked out.

Dang fool, Adam thought, don't even know he's an idiot *because* his momma and pappy were cousins.

When they finished their pie they said goodbye to the Cahill sisters and went outside.

"Well, gents," Bat said, "we've got a problem."

"What's that?" Short asked.

"There's two of them," Bat said, "and three of us."

"Seems to me," Short said, "they both kind of had eyes for Clint. What do you think, Clint?"

"For Clint?" Bat asked, before his friend could answer. "I don't think you were looking where I was looking, Luke. That Kitty couldn't take her eyes off of me."

"Now Bat," Short said, "we all know what a fine opinion you have of yourself as a ladies' man, but the fact is—"

"Are you saying you're more of a ladies' man than I am?" Bat asked.

"Hell, no . . ." Short said.

"I didn't think so."

"I'm satisfied just being a better poker player than you are," Short said. "Seems to me the ladies' man around here is Clint."

"Now, Luke—"

"You're a better poker player than me?" Bat asked.

"I'm glad you agree with me," Short said.

Bat looked at Clint.

"Are you hearing this?"

"I heard."

"What have you got to say about this?"

"You're both better poker players than me," Clint said, "so I'll just stay out of it."

Bat looked at Short and said, "You got an extra thousand in the bank, right?"

"That's right."

"You willing to put it up?"

"Head to head?"

"Unless Clint wants to play."

They both looked at him.

"I won't play," Clint said, "but I'll deal."

"You interested?" Bat asked Short.

"I'm interested."

"Then let's go."

"After you," Short said, "since I don't know the way to the saloon."

"You just follow me," Bat said, "and you and your money will soon be parting company."

Clint followed them both as they headed for the saloon, glad that they had gotten into one of their arguments about who the better poker player was, so that he didn't have to argue with Bat about who the bigger ladies' man was.

TWELVE

As is common with a head-to-head poker game the money gets passed back and forth across the table until both players are close to even after a few hours.

"Why not play, if you're going to deal?" Bat asked Clint.

"Hey," Clint said, "it's your grudge match."

"It's no grudge match," Bat said. "I'm just trying to prove a point to my friend here."

"Well," Clint said, "the point you've proved so far is that you're both about even."

"Sure," Bat said, "when it's just the two of us, but throw in some other players and see what happens."

"Like what happened last night?" Clint asked.

"What happened last night?" Short asked.

"Oh," Bat said, "we didn't tell you about our little adventure?"

"No," Short said. "Tell me about it. Maybe it'll be more interesting than this game."

By the time they were done Short was shaking his head.

"What's the matter?" Bat asked.

"Small stakes," Short said, "it just ain't worth it."

"We were just passing the time."

"People who play for small stakes can't afford to lose," Short said. "They should never play at all."

"You've got a point, Luke," Clint said.

Clint had played small stakes before, especially when trying to kill time, and it always ended badly. There were always bad losers in penny ante poker games. Of course, there were bad loser in high stakes games, too, but they generally got weeded out early, and they didn't wait outside with guns to get their money back.

"Anybody for another beer?" Clint asked.

"Me," Bat said.

"God, yes," Short agreed.

"I'll get 'em."

Bat picked up the cards and said, "Let me deal a few hands."

"Oh sure," Short said, good-naturedly, "that'll keep the game nice and honest."

Clint went to the bar and ordered three beers from Caleb Cahill.

"So, when are you fellas gonna start lookin' for the money?" Caleb asked, as he set the three mugs down.

"We're not," Clint said.

"But I thought you was here about the money?"

"We never said that," Clint replied. "Everybody else has said that, but not us."

"Ain't you interested?"

"Not in a myth."

"Who told you it was a myth?"

"Isn't it?"

"Mister," Caleb said, leaning his elbows on the bar, "that money is around here someplace."

"Then why haven't you and your family found it?" Clint asked.

"That's simple," Caleb said, straightening now. "We ain't smart enough. It'll take three smart fellas like you to find it."

"Well," Clint said, collecting the mugs, "these three smart fellas aren't going to be looking."

"Why not?" Caleb asked. "What else is there to do?"

Well, Clint thought as he walked back to the table, Caleb probably had a point there.

"Where would we ever start?" Short asked when Clint told his friends about Caleb's comments. "Do we know where these Cahill brothers were living when they buried it?"

"No," Clint said.

"Do we even know if they did actually bury it?" Bat said.

"What do you mean?" Clint asked.

"Maybe the money's under a floorboard somewhere."

"Or in a cave," Short said.

"Well," Clint said, "I'm not about to start ripping up floorboards. The myth says—according to the sheriff, anyway—that the money was buried."

Bat sat forward and asked, "Are you really planning on looking for it?"

"No," Clint said, "I'm just making conversation."

"It might be an interesting mental exercise," Short

said. "I mean, trying to figure out the best place to hide some money."

"Maybe," Bat said, "but why would these Cahill brothers even want to hide it from their family?"

"Maybe they wanted them to earn it," Clint said. "You know, get their hands dirty a bit."

"Then why not make it easier to find?" Bat asked.

"Maybe," Short said, "they simply underestimated how smart their own sons and daughters would be when they got older."

"And when was this money buried, anyway?" Bat asked. "After all, the oldest of these Cahills looks fifty. If he was a kid when the money was buried . . . we could be talking forty years!"

"What if the money's not even good anymore when it's found?" Short asked.

"You mean . . . like Confederate money?" Bat asked.

"Or just . . . rotted away."

"You'd think they'd be smart enough to wrap it in . . . something," Bat said.

Clint sat back, regarded his two friends, and said, "You'd think."

THIRTEEN

"How much longer are you fellas going to stay?" Short asked Clint and Bat later in the evening.

"Well," Clint said, "we *had* decided one more day without finding out anything, but since you've only just arrived . . ."

". . . we can extend it another day," Bat finished.

"I appreciate that," Short said. "I'd like to give my horse a day's rest, at least."

At that point the doors to the saloon opened and the sheriff walked in. He went directly to the bar, exchanged a few words with his cousin, and then got himself a beer. With the mug in hand he came walking over to the table where the three friends were seated.

During the course of the evening more and more of the other tables had been occupied, and now the place was nearly full and all eyes were on the four of them.

"Evenin', gents," Rupert Cahill said.

"Sheriff," Clint greeted.

"See you added one more person to your, uh . . . you've added another person."

51

"Sheriff," Bat said, "meet Luke Short. Luke, Sheriff Cahill."

"I heard of you, Mr. Short," Cahill said. "It's an honor to have you in our town."

"Thanks, Sheriff," Short said. "It's a . . . nice, quiet little place you have here."

"I like to keep it that way," Cahill said. "You boys decided how much longer you're gonna stay?"

"Probably another day," Clint said. "Luke only just arrived, and he wants to give his horse a chance to rest. We'll probably all be leaving together day after tomorrow."

"Ah."

"Unless something comes up," Bat added.

"Like what?"

Bat shrugged.

"Something can always come up to ruin your plans, Sheriff," Bat observed. "You never can tell."

"Well, that's true," the sheriff said. "Ya never can."

He stood there awkwardly for a moment, as if waiting for an invitation to sit, then shuffled his feet when it didn't come.

"Well," he said, "just thought I'd check in with you boys."

"We appreciate being looked after, Sheriff," Clint said.

"Have a good evenin'," Cahill said, and withdrew to the bar. There he and his cousin exchanged some heated words, and then the lawman downed his beer and stormed out.

"Somebody's not happy," Clint said.

"What do you suppose that was about?" Bat asked.

"Maybe it's got something to do with him being a cousin, and not a brother," Clint said.

"Maybe he's got brothers of his own," Luke said.

"Maybe," Clint said, "but I get the feeling this town is run by the three brothers we've met . . . Caleb here, Adam at the hotel and . . ."

"The liveryman," Bat said, "what's his name? Harley."

"That's it," Clint said. "Harley."

"Well," Short said, "they sure didn't seem to be getting along."

"Maybe he wasn't supposed to be talking to us," Bat suggested.

Clint looked around the room and as he did heads turned and eyes looked away.

"What if it's just the three of us?" he asked.

"Then they've got us here," Short said, "they should go ahead and make their move."

"Yeah," Clint said, "whatever that move is."

FOURTEEN

They decided to go back to their hotel rooms and get some sleep. Short, in particular, since he had ridden most of the day, was ready to turn in. Bat and Clint figured it was better than just sitting around.

When they reached the lobby Adam Cahill was still behind the desk.

"You the only one who works around here?" Clint asked.

"My hotel," Cahill said, "I do all the work. You three fellas decide if you're gonna look for the money or not?"

"We're not myth hunters," Bat said.

"Ain't a myth," Adam Cahill said.

"Well then, you and your family should look for it," Clint said. "After all, it's your inheritance."

"We've looked," the man said. "We looked for years, and then we got tired of looking and we decided just to live."

"Sounds like a good plan," Short said. "My plan, right now, is to get some sleep. Goodnight."

"I'll walk up with you, Luke," Bat said. "In case you need help getting all the way to the top."

"Like I'd ever need your help . . ." Short shot back as the two men started up the stairs.

Clint decided to stay in the lobby a while and talk to Adam Cahill. It struck him that this was the man who was in charge of the family.

"Saw your cousin earlier tonight."

"Got lots of cousins," Adam Cahill said. "Which one?"

"The sheriff."

There was a moment's hesitation and then he said, "Oh, him. What'd he want?"

"Well, I think maybe he wanted to sit with us," Clint said.

"You didn't invite him?"

"No."

"Good," Cahill said. "He's probably real impressed with the three of you, seein' who you are and all."

"And you're not impressed?"

"Oh, I'm impressed," the hotel owner said. "I just don't make a big deal out of it."

"Well, that's good," Clint said. "I don't like it when people make a big deal. I don't like all the attention."

"I'm sorry about my cousin, then," Adam said. "I'll talk to him."

"No need," Clint said. "I think he took the hint. Besides, he and your brother Caleb had some words afterward."

"An argument?"

"I don't know," Clint said. "We weren't close

enough to hear, but it looked like a pretty heated exchange."

"Yeah, well," the other man said, "those two never did get along."

"And what about Harley? He get along with the sheriff?"

"Harley gets along with everybody," Adam said. "He's a real easygoing type."

"Your sisters seem real nice."

"They are," Adam said. "Kate's a great cook."

"She does all the cooking?"

"Oh, yeah," the other man said. "Kate's the cook, Kitty's the waitress. That's the way they got it worked out."

"What about the other businesses in town?"

"Ain't too many," Adam said. "We own the general store. It's run by my cousin Jed."

"Is he the sheriff's brother?"

"No," Adam said, "Rupert's got no brothers. Jed, he's like a second cousin."

"And Rupert?"

"He was my uncle's only boy."

"Any sisters for Rupert?"

"One," Adam said. "Her name's Edna."

"What does she do in town?"

"Not a whole lot," Adam said. "Cooks for Rupert, I think. They share a little house on the edge of town."

"And where do the rest of you live?"

"We got places."

"What about—"

"How come you're all of a sudden so interested in my family?" Adam Cahill asked.

"It's a big family," Clint said. "I never had a family of any kind. I'm always curious about big families, about how they get along with one another."

"We get along okay," Adam said. "Didn't have a ma and a pa?"

"I suppose," Clint said, "but I never knew them."

"That's too bad," Adam said, "but at least your pa didn't go and bury somethin' where you can't find it."

"Well," Clint said, "that's true enough."

"Gettin' late," Adam said. "Thinkin' of turnin' in, myself."

"Who will man the desk when you do?"

"Nobody," Adam said. "Don't expect nobody to come checkin' in in the middle of the night. If they do though, all they gotta do is holler. I'll hear 'em soon enough."

Apparently, Adam's "place" to sleep was in the building.

"Okay, then," Clint said, "I'll bid you good night."

"You ain't checkin' out in the mornin', are ya? Any of ya?" Adam asked.

"No," Clint said, "we'll be around at least another day."

"That's good," Adam said.

"Why's that?"

"I can use the business," the man said. "I could always use the business."

FIFTEEN

Clint had spent many, many nights in hotels, and had had many, many knocks at his hotel doors. Some nights it was a friend, others it was somebody with a gun trying to blow his head off. Other nights it was a woman. Those nights in particular he didn't mind so much being awakened abruptly.

On this night when the knock came at the door it was soft and tentative, then more insistent. He supposed he had heard the first knock, but it hadn't prompted him from bed, as the second one did. He grabbed his gun from his holster, which he had hanging on the bedpost, and padded barefoot to the door.

"Who is it?"

"It's Kate," came the whispered reply, "from the café?"

Idly, he wondered if he had even heard her speak during their two visits there.

He unlocked the door and opened it. She was still wearing the plain dress she had been wearing at the café, and he could smell both the natural scent of her

59

body, and the smells of the cooking she must have
done all day.

"Can I come in?" she asked.

"It's late," he said. "Do you want to be seen going
into a man's room late at night?"

She looked both ways in the hall and then said,
"There's no one out here to see me, and nobody was
in the lobby. If you open the door soon enough, I think
I can avoid being seen."

He opened the door and she stepped inside, closing
the door behind her. When she turned to face him she
saw the gun in his hand.

"I don't have a weapon," she said, spreading her
arms, which caused her full breasts to lift. "You can
search me if you want."

"Sorry," he said, "force of habit."

He walked back to the bedpost and holstered the
gun, then turned to face her. He was not only barefoot,
but bare-chested, as well. He wondered if her sister was
down the hall knocking on either Bat's or Luke Short's
door. If she was, his money was on Bat. While Luke
was the better gambler—not something Bat would ever
admit—Bat did better with the ladies.

"Kate," he said, "I didn't expect to see you. I mean,
I—"

"Were you expecting Kitty?"

"I wasn't expecting either—"

"We talked about who should come, and I won," she
said, reaching behind her, which *really* caused her
breasts to lift up and present themselves to him, "because I'm the oldest."

"Kate, what are you—"

"Most of the men in this town are either ugly," she said, "or kin. In some cases both. You're the first good-looking, interesting man to come to Bended Knee in a long time, and I don't intend to let you go to waste."

She undid her dress in the back and let it fall to the floor. Her body was a myriad of curves and shadows. Her skin was pale, her breasts full and heavy, with large nipples. The light from the lamp gave her body a golden glow. The tangle of hair between her thighs seemed to shine.

"I hope you don't mind aggressive women," she said.

"In this instance," he said, reaching for her, "I suppose I can make an exception."

Outside, in the hall, Kitty watched from the stairway as her sister knocked on Clint's door. When it opened and Kate stepped in, Kitty waited for the door to close then hurried down the hall to Bat Masterson's room and knocked on his door. She and her sister *had* sort of fought over Clint Adams, but Kate had reasoned that there would probably be another night, and as the older sister she should go first with Clint. She gave Kitty her pick of the other two men, and Kitty chose Bat because he was prettier than the other man.

Clint pulled Kate to him, crushing her breasts against his chest. His hands roamed over her back and came to rest covering her impressive buttocks. Her skin was smooth and firm all over.

She moaned as she felt his erection against the front of his pants. She went to her knees and frantically un-

buttoned his pants, pulling them down around his ankles. He had also removed his boots earlier, so all he
had to do was step out of the Levi's and his underwear,
and he was naked.

She gave all her attention to his swollen penis. She
cooed to it, licked it, bit it, dragged her nails along the
underside, weighed his testicles in her palm and then,
finally, took him into her hot, wet mouth and began to
avidly suck him.

"Jesus," he said, his legs almost buckling as she
worked the length of him in and out of her mouth,
squeezing the cheeks of his butt in her hands at the
same time.

"God," she said, releasing him, "you taste so
good . . ."

"Come up here so I can taste you," he said, reaching
for her.

"No," she said, pushing him so that he fell onto the
bed on his back, "this is too good. I want to do this
for a while."

She crawled onto him and captured him in her
mouth again. The scent of her—food, sweat and now
her wetness—was a heady mix and the way she was
sucking him he wasn't sure he was going to be able to
last for a while.

But, with her help, he did. . . .

SIXTEEN

Clint awoke the next morning with Kate's warm body pressed up against his from behind. He could feel her solid breasts against his back and, with one leg tossed over him, he could feel her pubic patch pressing against him, giving off incredible heat. Then he realized what had awakened him: She had taken him in her hand and begun stroking him so that he was growing harder and harder.

"Good God, woman," he said, "can't you get enough?"

In his ear she said, "When you have gone without as long as I have, I'll let you answer that."

She continued to stroke him until he was near bursting, then flipped him on his back, mounted him and slid onto him neat as you please. She was so wet and hot that he gasped when she took him inside of her. She rode him that way, her head thrown back, as if she was in a hurry to get it over with, but he knew that wasn't the case. He knew that she was simply mindless in her pursuit of her own pleasure, because he had been like that many times himself. Sometimes you are concerned with not only your pleasure, but the pleasure of your partner. And then there are the other times, when all you care about is your own pleasure. That was where Kate was now, and he felt she was deserving.

So he bit his lip and fought the urge to finish as long as he could. Maybe if she had not used her hand on him to awaken him he could have lasted longer, but finally she gasped and began to convulse on top of him and he lost his battle and exploded just seconds after her . . .

"I have to open the café," Kate said a little later. He watched as she got dressed. She had awakened him early so they could have sex one more time before she went to work. That was what she had said. "Have sex." He liked her directness. A lot of women had pet names for what they did, but not her. She called it what it was.

"What about your sister, Kitty?"

"I expect she's down the hall with your friend Mr. Masterson."

"What, not with Luke Short?"

She smiled and said, "She thought Mr. Masterson was prettier."

"I'm sure he'll be happy to hear that."

Dressed, she turned to face him.

"Will you be leaving town today?"

"No," he said, "we're here until at least tomorrow. Will you be back tonight?"

"No," she said. "Kitty and I made a deal. Tonight is her turn."

"So I'm being passed back and forth between sisters?"

"It looks like that," she said. "Do you mind?"

"What if she wants to go back to Bat?"

"Well then, I guess you'll be stuck with me again."

"And if she comes here," he asked, "will you go to Bat's room?"

She thought a moment, then said, "I would feel sorry for Mr. Short, I think, because he got left out. I think I'd go to his room."

"Kate," Clint said, "can I ask you something before you leave?"

She sat in the only chair in the room, her hands clasped primly in her lap, and said, "Ask."

"You seem more educated than the rest of your family."

"Guilty, I'm afraid," she said. "I've been to school, but I came back to take care of my family."

"Did you come back because of the money?"

"The myth, you mean?"

"Do you believe it?" he asked. "Or *is* it a myth?"

"Who knows?" she asked. "My father and his brother were strange men. They could have buried some sort of treasure around here, hoping that one of their offspring would be smart enough to find it."

"The boys, you mean?"

"Of course, the boys," she said. "Papa never would have expected Kitty or me to find it, and Uncle Ezra never would have expected it of my cousin Edna— who's an idiot, by the way."

"The sheriff's sister?"

She nodded.

"Do you mean uneducated?"

"I mean an idiot, like Rupert."

"Why do you say that?"

"My aunt and uncle were first cousins," she said. "If I learned anything while I was away it's that you don't mix cousins and expect to come up with bright children."

"Was that . . . I mean, is that . . . what I mean is—"

"Yes," she said, "for a while my family did that sort of thing, but not my parents."

"What about your grandparents?"

"On my father's side, I think so, but not my mother's," she said. "Maybe I'd be smarter if—"

"That's silly," he said. "You're fine."

"Well," she said, "my cousin Rupert seems to think that Kitty would make a good wife for him."

"And what does Kitty think?"

"Unfortunately," she said, "she doesn't think it's as bad an idea as Adam and I do."

"Adam runs the hotel." He wasn't asking, he was reminding himself.

"Yes, and he's considered head of the family."

"And he's against it?"

"Thank God, yes," she said. "My brothers aren't all that educated, Clint, but Adam's pretty smart. I tried to get him to go to school when I did, but he wouldn't listen. Said he was too old."

"All your brothers seem to be older than you and your sister."

"We came along late in life," she said, "after all the bank and train robbing had stopped and Pa and Uncle Ezra had settled down."

"Did your brothers ever think about following in your father's footsteps?" he asked.

"You mean bringing back the Cahill Gang? They've talked about it once or twice."

"And?"

"They'd get caught first time out," she said. "None of them is as smart as Pa was, and he did all the planning."

"Not even Adam?"

"He could have been," she said. "He could have been the smartest one of us all, but . . ."

She shrugged and stood up.

"I've got to go to work." She walked to the door, then turned. "I'm not coming near the bed, because if I did you could convince me to stay."

"I could?"

"Well," she said, "your body could. Come by later and I'll feed you."

"Count on it."

She smiled and then went out the door, leaving behind all of her mixed scents.

SEVENTEEN

Clint got washed and dressed and walked down the hall to Bat's room. He knocked and Bat answered immediately. He looked a lot happier than he had been looking the day before.

"Looks like you had a good night," Clint said.

"You, too?"

Clint nodded.

"I understand we might be traded off tonight."

"Or," Bat said, "one of us might lose out to Luke."

They looked at each other for a moment, then both said, "Naw!"

"Let's go wake him up for breakfast, though," Bat said, stepping into the hall and closing his door. He had traded in his trail clothes from the day before for his nattier attire, a black suit and a boiled white shirt, and a bowler. Clint didn't say anything about Bended Knee being a little small for those kind of clothes. Bat dressed for himself, and for no one else.

"But let's not rub it in, huh?" Clint asked.

"Aw, why not?" Bat asked. "What's the use of

spending the night with a wild, willing blonde if you
can't—"

"Come on, Bat."

"Well," Bat said, "at least you know about it."

They walked to Short's door and knocked. He answered, dressed and ready to go.

"I thought we'd have to wake you," Bat said.

"You did," Short said, "both of you with your all-
night and early morning rutting sessions."

"You heard us?" Bat asked.

"These walls are like paper, my friend," Luke Short
said, closing his door and stepping into the hall. "Bat,
what were you doing to that girl to make her agree
with you so vehemently?"

"Luke," Bat said, "if I have to tell you that—"

"Never mind," Short said, "I was joking. Are the
two ladies in question going to be able to cook breakfast?"

"Oh, yeah," Clint said, "I don't think that's going to
be a problem."

"Good," Short said, "I'd hate to think that my appetite would have to suffer to enhance your love lives.
Shall we go?"

"By all means," Bat said. He grinned at Clint behind
Short's back and Clint knew Bat was feeling very satisfied with himself. He wondered how satisfied his
friend would feel if Kate decided to spend the next
night with Luke Short after all.

Sheriff Rupert Cahill was in a doorway across the
street from the hotel early that morning, in time to see
Kate and Kitty Cahill leaving the hotel. He frowned.

He didn't mind Kate having some fun with the visitors, but Kitty was his woman—or she would be soon. He couldn't have his woman visiting other men's hotel rooms.

It was Kate who spotted him across the street and, without telling Kitty, she doubled back and confronted him in his doorway.

"Rupert Cahill, what are you doing snooping around here?"

"I'm doin' my job."

"You're spying on Kitty."

"What if I am?" he demanded. "Ain't that part of my job, lookin' out for family?"

"No, it isn't," Kate said. "Rupert, I thought Adam warned you about sniffing around Kitty. I thought you understood."

"Well, I don't," he said, sulking.

"Well," she said, "you don't have to. Just stay away from her, stop spying on her or, cousin or no cousin, I'll put a bullet in you."

"Aw, Kate—"

"I will, Rupert," she said. "I swear."

He sulked some more, then muttered, "Can't shoot the sheriff."

"I will," she said, poking him in the side with a stiffened forefinger. "Right in the ass. Remember that."

She turned and left him there, still sulking, and he muttered, "That wouldn't be a ladylike thing to do."

EIGHTEEN

The three friends had breakfast at the café, being treated very special by the sisters, Kitty and Kate. There were other diners there, but no one got the special attention Clint, Bat and Luke Short got.

"See?" Bat said to Luke Short. "Stick with us and you get fed real well."

"I knew there was a reason I was friends with you clowns."

Clint insisted on paying the bill and then they left the café, stopping on the boardwalk just outside. There was a rider coming into town, and the three of them were transfixed.

"This might be it," Bat said.

"As soon as we see who he is," Clint said, "maybe it will be."

"Can you make him out?" Short asked.

"The way he sits his horse is not familiar," Bat said.

So they stood there and waited for him to get closer, and when he finally came into view they all looked at each other.

"Either of you know him?" Clint asked.

"No," Bat said.

"Never saw him before," Short said.

Clint shrugged and said, "Me, neither."

The rider in question was a man who appeared to be in his late thirties, dressed in dusty trail clothes, riding a small, gray colt and paying no attention to the three of them. He had a gun on his left hip, which might have been reason enough for them to remember him, as the number of left-handed guns in the west was not great.

They watched him go past and kept watching until he was out of sight—they assumed, on his way to the livery stable.

"Could just be some fella riding into town," Bat said. "May have nothing to do with us."

"The impression I get around here is that they don't get a lot of visitors," Clint said. "That's what makes the three of us unusual, and I guess that's what's going to make this fellow unusual, too."

"Maybe we should talk to him," Short said.

"Not our place," Clint said. "Let the sheriff check him out."

"What if it's him?" Bat said.

Clint and Short looked at him.

"I mean what if he's the guy who sent us the money, and the invitation?" Bat asked.

"Well," Clint said, after a moment, "if it *is* him, then we'll be hearing from him."

They went to the saloon and found it open. There was no one inside but the bartender/owner, Caleb.

"Welcome, gents," Caleb said. "My first customers of the day."

"It's a little early to be open, ain't it?" Bat asked.

"I own the place," Caleb said. "I make the rules. Beer?"

"You got any coffee?" Clint asked. "It's a little early for beer."

"On the house," Caleb said, "seein' as how you're my first customers."

"Beer sounds good," Luke Short said, and the others nodded.

Caleb lined the beers up on the bar and rather than take them to a table the three friends stood at the bar.

"Have one with us?" Clint asked.

"Don't mind if I do."

When Caleb also had a beer mug Clint asked, "You know a fellow who rides a little gray horse?"

"A gray horse?"

"That's right."

Caleb shrugged, but there was something in his eyes.

"Lots of folks ride gray horses," he said. "Why do you ask?"

"We saw a fella ride in just a little while ago," Bat said. "He's a stranger to us, but we thought you might know him."

"Reckon I'd have to see him before I can say," Caleb replied.

"Well," Clint said, "since this is the only saloon in town, I suppose you eventually will."

Clint could see that Caleb was nervous now, but he had no excuse to leave them to their beers. He was still drinking his, and there were still no other customers.

"So what about this myth?" Short asked.

"Huh?"

"The money your father and uncle supposedly hid," Bat said. "You have no idea where it might be?"

"Uh, no, none," Caleb said. "We, uh, looked, but Adam finally decided we should give up."

"Why would he do that?" Bat asked.

"He said we was wasting our lives."

"Maybe," Short said, "Adam found it, and that's why he wanted the rest of you to stop looking."

Clint looked at Short, wondering if the man was joshing, or if he was trying to stir something up.

"Huh?" Caleb said.

"You and your brothers and sisters never considered that?" Bat asked, joining in. "That maybe one of you found it and didn't tell the others?"

Caleb screwed up his face and said, "Now, why would one of us wanna go and do that?"

"Because not all families are close," Bat said.

"Well," Caleb said, "ours is."

"How about—" Short started, but now Caleb had himself a reason to leave them.

"I gotta go," he said, sounding hurt and insulted. "You fellas finish your beers."

"What if somebody else comes in?" Bat asked as Caleb came around the bar and headed for the door.

"Nobody will," Caleb said, and left.

"I think you fellas just might have stirred something up," Clint said, and they clinked mugs.

NINETEEN

The new arrival in town did not go to the livery stable. Nor was he ignorant of the three men who were watching him ride down the street. Once he was out of their sight he directed his horse down an alley and came up to the hotel from behind. He dismounted, secured his horse and entered through the back door. He made his way down a hall that led to a curtained doorway. On the other side of the doorway was the front desk, with Adam Cahill standing behind it. He parted the curtains just enough to make sure there was no one else around, and called Adam's name.

Adam Cahill whirled around at the sound of his name, eyes wide. When he saw the man, he hurried down the hallway and pulled the curtains closed behind him.

"When did you get to town?" he demanded.

"Just now."

"Did they see you?"

"Oh, yeah."

"Is that wise?"

"None of them knew who I was, and I didn't acknowledge their presence," the man said.

"But . . . did they know you?"

"I doubt it," the man said. "Right now they're wracking their brains, trying to figure out who I am, or if I'm even involved with sending them the money and inviting them here. Just because they don't know me doesn't mean I'm also a stranger in town."

"They're gonna ask around."

"Sure they are."

"But they'll ask my brothers," Adam said, "and that idiot, Rupert."

"So?"

"So?" Adam repeated. "My brothers will get nervous."

"They won't give anything away. They know better."

"Maybe not on purpose, but—"

"Adam!"

The voice startled Adam, but not the other man.

"That's Caleb."

"Get him back here."

Adam nodded and went through the curtains. Caleb charged the desk when he saw Adam.

"They're in the saloon."

"Caleb," Adam said, "come around—"

"But they're askin' me questions."

"Caleb!" Adam said. He didn't want his brother to sound panicked, not with the man behind the curtain listening. "Come in the back."

"But Adam—"

"Come in the back!" Adam snapped. "We'll talk there."

Caleb opened his mouth to say something else but the look Adam gave him caused him to shut it again. He went around the desk and followed his brother through the curtains. He stopped short when he saw the other man standing in the hallway.

"W-what's he doin' here?" he asked.

"I'm here to check on you boys," the man said. "I want to make sure you're all doing your part."

"We are," Adam said. "Don't worry about that."

"Oh, I'm not worried," the man said. He looked at Caleb, who was scared to death of him. "Do I look worried, Caleb?"

"N-no," Caleb said. "You don't look worried."

"Good. Caleb, my horse is out back. Be a good fella and take it over to the livery for me, will you?"

"S-sure," Caleb said, "sure I will."

He turned to go through the curtains.

"Use the back door," the man said.

"Right," Caleb said, "the back door."

"And give my best to your brother Harley, will you?"

"S-sure."

Caleb hurried down the hall as fast as he could without actually breaking into a run.

"Can't understand why he's so afraid of me," the man said. He turned to Adam. "Can you?"

"Sure," Adam said. "You're a killer."

"You're not afraid of me, are you, Adam?"

"Sure I am."

"But I thought we were friends."

"You'd kill me in a second," Adam said. "I don't think that makes us friends."

"Well," the man said, "in any case, I'm going to need a room down here."

"You're gonna stay here? Where they are?"

"As long as I'm not on the same floor with them, why not?"

"But . . . the only room down here is mine."

The man smiled and said, "I'll take it."

Adam pressed his lips together, then said, "All right."

"Clean it up for me, will you?" the man asked. "You can have one of your sisters do that."

"Yes, all right."

"And how are your sisters, anyway?" the man asked. "Still as beautiful as ever?"

"Stay away from my sisters, or—"

"I'd like my meals prepared by them while I'm here," the man said, cutting Adam off. "And I'd like one of them to deliver a tray to me each day. Can you have them do that, Adam?"

"If you touch one of my sisters—"

"I thought you said you were afraid of me."

"I am," Adam said, "but that don't mean I won't tell you what I think of you."

"But that might make me take that second you were talking about," the man said. "The one it would take me to kill you?"

"I don't care."

"You don't care if I kill you?"

"No."

The man smiled.

"But you care about your brothers, right?"

Adam compressed his lips again.

"And your sisters."

Adam felt his face growing warm.

"I'm not asking for so much, am I?" the man said. "A clean room, some hot meals?"

"No," Adam finally said, "I suppose not."

The man smiled, stepped forward and patted Adam's cheek.

"Just think what's in it for you and your family when this is all over, Adam," he said. "Just keep thinkin' about that."

TWENTY

In the absence of a bartender Clint drew three more beers and this time they did take them over to a table.

"Say one thing for Caleb," Clint said. "He knows the town. Nobody else has come in."

"He was Caleb?" Bat asked. "I thought Caleb ran the livery."

"No, Harley runs the livery," Clint said.

"I thought that was Adam," Bat said.

"Adam runs the hotel," Clint said patiently.

"And who's the sheriff?" Short asked.

Together, Clint and Bat said, "Rupert!"

Short shook his head.

"I'm never gonna get them straight."

"Neither am I," Bat said, "but at least I know Kitty from Kate."

Short gave his friend a look and said, "I'm not even gonna ask how."

Bat looked at the door.

"I never saw a bartender take off and leave a bar *un*tended," he said.

"No," Short said, "neither have I."

"You boys put a scare into him, I guess," Clint said.

Bat looked at both of them. "Do you suppose it really never occurred to him that one of his brothers might find the money and keep it all?"

"I guess not," Clint said.

"Would Ed do that?" Short asked.

Bat hesitated.

"Well," Short said, "if you have to think about it . . ."

"That's different," Bat said. "It would depend on the circumstances."

"Same as these," Short said. "You and Ed are in the same town together, dying to get out."

"Ed would share."

"You're sure of that?"

"I am. You fellas aren't even my brothers and I'd share with you," Bat said. "And it would never occur to me that you wouldn't share with me."

Short looked at Clint and asked, "Don't you hate being predictable?"

"More than you know."

They sipped their beer in silence, alone with their own thoughts for a few moments.

"Okay," Bat said, breaking the silence, "the fella who rode in today has nothing to do with this. What do we do then?"

"Well," Clint said, "if nobody else rides in today and we don't hear anything from him, I'll be riding out of here in the morning."

"Sure is quiet around here," Short said. "A man could get used to quiet."

•

"You stay, then," Bat said. "I'll be riding out with Clint."

"I said a man could get used to it," Short said. "I didn't say I was that man. I'm with you fellas."

"Okay," Bat said, sitting back, "then I guess the question now is, what do we do in the meantime?"

They all exchanged a glance, and then Bat smiled and took a fresh deck of cards from his pocket.

"I'm tellin' ya, Harley," Caleb said, "he's over at the hotel right now with Adam."

"And where are those other fellers?" Harley asked.

"In the saloon."

"A-drinkin' yore beer?"

"I guess."

"For free?"

"I give 'em one free each."

"But you ain't there," Harley said, "and what's gonna happen after they finish that one beer each?"

Caleb stared at his brother for a moment, then said, "Shit," and started running back to the saloon.

TWENTY-ONE

Kate entered the hotel carrying a tray of food. When Adam saw her he said, "It's about time. He's been yellin' for his food."

"Let him yell," she said, walking toward the desk. "Maybe you're afraid of him, but I'm not."

"You're too smart not to be afraid of him, Kate," Adam said. "Come in, he wants you to bring it to him."

She set the tray down on the desk and said, "Can't you?"

"He wants you or Kitty."

"Well, forget that," Kate said, picking the tray up again. "I'll do it. I'm not letting him near Kitty."

She came around the desk and Adam held the curtain aside for her.

"Where is he?"

"My room."

"Your room? Why did you give him your room?"

"Because he wanted it."

"What else would you give him just because he wanted it, Adam?" she asked.

"Never mind, Kate," her older brother said. "Just bring him his damn food. Do you want me to knock on the door for you?"

"I can knock, Adam," she said. "Don't worry about me."

But, as Adam watched his sister walk down the hall, balance the tray on one hand and knock on the door, he did worry about her. When the door opened she stepped inside. When it closed Adam made his way down the hall and pressed his ear to the door. He wanted to be in position to help his sister, if she needed it.

"It's nice to see you again, Kate," the man said, "although I was hoping to see Kitty."

"She's busy."

"I thought you were the cook," he said, as she set the tray down on the dresser. "I thought with you in the kitchen she'd be bringing the food over."

"Well," she said, turning to face him, "I brought it. Just leave the tray outside the door when you've finished. I'll pick it up later."

"Or maybe Kitty will pick it up?"

Kate started for the door and said, "I'll get it."

As she went past him he grabbed her arm, halting her progress toward the door.

"Why are you in such a hurry?"

"We're real busy at the café."

"Too busy to come and see an old friend?"

She turned her head and gave him a cold stare.

"When were we ever friends?"

He touched his heart and said, "You wound me."

"For that to be true," she said, "you would have to have a heart."

He released his hold on her arm and stepped back from her.

"You give off a cold chill, Kate," he said. "It could freeze a man to death."

"I only wish you were right."

He compressed his lips in annoyance, but then decided she wasn't worth it. The object of his desires—his true desires—was Kitty, not Kate.

"All right," he said. "I won't try anymore. You can go. When I'm finished I'll put the tray in the hall."

"Fine," she said, and left, almost knocking over her brother Adam.

"You're listening at keyholes now?" she demanded.

"Only to see if you needed me," he said.

"Well, as you can see, I didn't."

She started down the hall to the curtained doorway and he walked along with her.

"You take a lot of chances when you talk to him like that, Kate," he advised her.

"I don't care," she said. "I don't like him, and I'm not afraid of him. I want him to stay away from Kitty. In fact, I want him to stay away from our whole family."

At the doorway she stopped and faced her brother.

"Why do you put up with him, Adam?"

"He's going to help us get what we want."

"And what's that?"

"You'll find out."

"I'll fi—Oh, wait."

"Why don't you go back to work now?"

He stepped through the curtain and took up his position behind the desk.

"Adam," she said, following him, but moving around to the front of the desk, "not that buried money."

He didn't answer.

"You can't believe in that myth," she said. "Not you."

She put her hand on his but he pulled it away abruptly.

"Do you want to run a café all your life?" he asked. "I know I don't want to run a hotel for the rest of mine."

"But that old myth—"

"We'll find out once and for all if it is a myth."

"With his help?"

"Yes," Adam said, "with his help."

"At what price, Adam?" she asked. "Tell me that. At what price?"

Adam stared back at his sister and said with feeling, "At any price."

TWENTY-TWO

Abruptly, in the middle of the afternoon, Bat and Luke Short decided to go for a ride.

"Want to come?" Bat asked Clint.

"No," Clint said, "I'm just going to hang around town. Good luck to the two of you, though, in finding the money when the whole family hasn't been able to do it in years."

Both men looked chagrined but Bat said, "We're just going to take a little innocent look around."

"We'd split it with you, anyway," Short said.

"I know," Clint said. "I meant it when I wished you luck."

"We'll see you later tonight," Bat said, and the two men left. Although Clint considered Bat to be his best friend he somehow envied the relationship Bat seemed to have with Luke Short. Clint felt a special kinship with Bat, and Luke Short and, to the same extent, Wyatt Earp, and often wondered how those men felt about him. Loyal to their friendship, yes, but Clint felt loyalty to some people without there being a close friendship.

And then there was his friendship with Rick Hartman, which seemed to exist on a whole other level. He had things in common with Bat Masterson, Luke Short and Wyatt Earp that didn't exist in his friendship with Hartman.

Clint wondered if it was an asset or a hindrance for him to feel he had a close friendship with more than one man? He then shook his head and wondered what his problem was. Any of those men would come to his aid no matter when or where he needed it, and he'd do the same for them. That was all any of them needed to know.

For him to be sitting around examining friendships, as well as the very word, meant he had way too much time on his hands. Maybe he should have gone treasure hunting with Bat and Luke Short, after all.

He left the saloon and decided to take a walk around town, forgetting that such a walk would not take long at all. Eventually, he found himself at the livery stable and decided to check in on Eclipse.

As he entered the stable Harley Cahill turned and the two men spotted each other at the same time.

"Oh," Cahill said, "uh, I didn't hear ya come in. Do you need your horse?"

"No," Clint said, "I just came to look in on him."

"Well, go ahead," Harley Cahill said. "I'll just go on with my work, then."

"Sure, go ahead."

Clint moved into the livery and found Eclipse's stall. He stepped in, patted the horse's neck and spoke to him. Unlike his big black gelding, Duke, who would respond to the sound of his voice as if he understood every word, this horse had not yet developed such a habit. This was the reason that Clint, when they were on the trail, spent a lot of time speaking to Eclipse, so that the horse would get used to hearing the sound of his voice. He wanted the animal to not only come to know it, but to trust it, as well.

It was while he was doing this that he looked at the stall across from Eclipse's and saw the little gray he and Bat and Luke Short had seen a man ride in on earlier that day.

When he was finished with Eclipse he stepped from the stall and looked around. He didn't see Cahill anywhere so he stepped across to the stall of the gray horse. He examined the animal quickly, found him very sound but could find no brands on it. A saddle was sitting nearby, but no saddlebags. There was nothing here to tell him about the horse's rider.

Unless . . .

He found Harley Cahill out behind the barn, using a pitchfork to transfer some hay onto the back of a buckboard.

"Can I talk to you a minute?" he asked.

Harley Cahill turned, again startled by Clint's appearance. He held the pitchfork in an aggressive manner for a few moments, and then relaxed.

"Uh, sure," he said, "what about?"

"That gray horse inside."

There was a hitch in Cahill's movements for just a moment, just enough to be a giveaway.

"I don't know nothin' about it."

"You know who rode in on it?"

"A fella."

"What kind of fella?"

"Just a fella."

"A stranger?" Clint asked. "Or does he live around here?"

"Look, mister," Cahill said, clearly uncomfortable with the line of questioning, "I got work to do."

Clint was going to press the issue, but decided not to. He felt he had the answer to his question.

"Okay," Clint said, "you go on about your work."

Harley Cahill turned his back on Clint, who decided to walk around the stable, then back through it. While Harley had not told him so in so many words, Clint now felt sure that the man on the gray horse was no stranger to Bended Knee or to the Cahills.

TWENTY-THREE

Clint went to the hotel and found Adam Cahill in his customary position behind the desk. With nothing better to do he had decided to continue to try and find out who the man on the gray horse was.

"Afternoon, Mr. Adams," Cahill said. "Somethin' I can do for you?"

"A man rode into town on a gray horse today, Mr. Cahill," Clint said. "I was wondering if he was staying here?"

Cahill frowned.

"I don't know what color horse folks ride in on, Mr. Adams," Cahill said, "but I can tell you that only you and your two friends have registered in the past few days. And for sure nobody registered today."

"Is there anyplace else he could stay in town?"

"Well, I guess that would depend if he had any friends in town," Cahill said.

"So you don't know a man who rides a gray horse?"

" 'fraid I don't."

"Okay, then," Clint said. "Thanks."

•   •   •

As Clint Adams went out the door Adam Cahill let go a relieved sigh. It just wasn't time, yet, for the Gunsmith and the man he called The Man on the Gray Horse to meet.

Still, the man should know that Clint Adams was here looking for him. Cahill left the desk and went into the back hall.

Clint waited outside for Adam Cahill to leave the desk, which he did almost immediately. He knew there was no use, but he wanted to get a look at the register, anyway. As Cahill had said, nobody had registered since Luke Short the day before.

Clint heard voices in the back hall. He went around behind the desk and peered through the curtains. He saw Adam Cahill standing in the hall, speaking to someone who was standing in a room. The door was open, but no part of the man in the room was showing. The conversation ended, with Clint having missed all of it, and the door closed. As Cahill started back down the hall Clint hurried out from behind the desk and left the hotel. He'd seen an empty food tray on the floor outside the room, and he figured there was only one place it would have come from.

He walked over to the café, which was busy—or as busy as a place could be in a small town like Bended Knee. Actually, it was pretty busy because, as far as Clint had been able to determine, there weren't that many other places in town to eat.

Kitty saw Clint come in and hurried over to him.

"Hungry again already?"

"No, not really," Clint said. "Actually, I wanted to talk to you or your sister for a moment."

"What about?"

"Did you take a tray of food over to the hotel today for a guest, Kitty?" he asked.

"No, I didn't," Kitty said, "but I saw Kate leave with a tray."

"Who was it for?"

"Well, that's the odd thing," Kitty said. "She wouldn't tell me who it was for."

"You asked her?"

"Straight out," Kitty said. "And she straight out told me it didn't matter who it was for and I should get back to work. She snapped at me!"

"Is that unusual?"

"Real unusual," Kitty said, pouting. "She never talks to me that way. Hurt my feelings."

Clint put his hand on her arm and rubbed it, a soothing gesture he was only partially aware of.

"Well, maybe she'll tell me," Clint said, "and then I can tell you."

"Would you?"

"Sure."

"But . . . she can't talk to you now. She's at the stove."

"Well, I'll come back later, when it's not as busy."

"Okay," Kitty said. "Should I tell her you were here?"

"No," Clint said, "that's okay. I'll just stop by."

"See you later, then," she said, brightly, her hurt feelings apparently forgotten.

• • •

Clint left the café, convinced now that the man on the
gray horse was, indeed, connected with the Cahills, and
maybe with the reason he and Bat and Luke Short were
summoned here. Nobody was talking though—nobody
who knew anything. Both Harley and Adam Cahill had
lied to him, but Kitty knew nothing. He was sure of
that. Kate had to know, though, if she delivered the
tray of food. The question was, would she tell him?

TWENTY-FOUR

The man who had arrived on the gray horse was not concerned that Clint Adams was asking about him. In truth, he would have been disappointed otherwise. Of the three men it was Clint Adams he expected to figure out who he was, and find him. Not that he was so much smarter than Masterson or Short, but he was the more stubborn of the three.

He stalked, hand on his gun. He was anxious to play the scenario out, but they were still waiting for one more player. He did not want to jump the gun and lose out. His revenge had to be complete, and had to be taken on all four men involved.

So although he felt like a caged animal he knew he had to stay in this room until all four men were in town. He was not hiding. That would imply that he was afraid—and the only fear he had was that his vengeance would not be complete.

And, to him, an incomplete vengeance would be like having no vengeance at all.

● ● ●

Adam Cahill stood behind the desk of his hotel, looking around the lobby. He hated this place. He hated
the hotel, and the town, and he hated the man who was
presently occupying his room, causing him to have to
sleep in one of the rooms in the hotel he hated.

It would all be worth it in the end, though. All he
had to do was help the man get what he wanted, and
then *he* would also get what he wanted.

It would all be worth it in the end—wouldn't it?

Kate Cahill slaved over the hot stove in her café, thinking about what her brother had said.

Did she want to do this forever?

Actually, to her surprise, the answer was yes. She
enjoyed the cooking, and she enjoyed serving her food
to people. However, she realized that what she hated
was having to do it here, in Bended Knee.

So maybe Adam was right. Maybe they had to do
what they had to do to get away from here.

Maybe in the end it *would* all be worth it.

Maybe.

Clint seated himself in front of the hotel, waiting for
Bat and Short to return. He felt certain that the Man
on the Gray Horse was somewhere in the building he
was leaning against. If he was a man of shorter pa-
tience he could probably storm in there and force him
to reveal himself. But while he was stubborn—he admitted that—he was not impatient. Besides, his two
friends would probably be angry with him if he did
anything without them.

He laughed to himself, thinking of his friends out

there searching for buried treasure. He himself had panned for gold, and mined for it and searched for buried treasure in Mexico. Who was he to criticize them for testing out a theory and seeing if they could find something?

After all, what else was there to do?

Bat and Luke Short rode in circles for a few hours before deciding to give up.

"No caves," Short said. "Caves are good to hide things in. The James Boys used caves."

"I don't think the Cahills were on the same level as Frank and Jesse, Luke."

"Probably not."

"It's probably all just a family story, anyway," Bat said.

"I didn't expect to find anything, anyway."

"Neither did I."

They looked at each other and started laughing.

"Makes us pretty dumb for being out here in the first place, doesn't it?" Bat asked.

"It sure does," Short said. "Clint is probably back in the saloon having another beer and laughing at us."

Suddenly, a look of concern crossed Bat's face.

"What is it?" Short asked.

"I just thought of something."

"What?"

"While we're out here riding around in circles," Bat said, "Clint is in town alone, with nobody to watch his back."

"Jesus," Short said, "we are stupid."

"Let's go," Bat said.

"Let's hope that nobody got the bright idea to go after one of us when we were alone."

"Shit," Short said, as they wheeled their horses around and pointed them back to town, "if anything's happened to him—"

"I know," Bat said, "I feel the same way."

"So let's stop talkin'," Short said, "and start ridin'."

TWENTY-FIVE

Clint returned to the café when he thought it would be less busy. Sure enough as he walked in, the last two customers were just walking out. There'd be time to talk to Kate until people started coming in for dinner.

"Hello?"

He waited a moment, then headed for the kitchen. Before he reached it, though, Kitty came walking out.

"Oh!" she said, jumping and putting her hand over her heart. "You startled me."

"I'm sorry, Kitty," he said. "I came back to talk to Kate."

"Oh, well, she's not here," she said, adopting a flirtatious manner now. She put her hands behind her back and pushed her chest out at him. Her breasts were large and firm and didn't need to be pushed out. "Maybe you could talk to me?"

"You said earlier that you didn't know who she had taken the food to at the hotel."

"Oh," she said. "Is that what this is about?"

"Yes. Where did she go?"

"Well . . . she said she had to go over to the hotel."

"Maybe I can catch her over there."

She grabbed his arm as he was about to leave.

"Is it so important that you can't spend a little time with me?" she asked.

Before he could answer she put her arms around him and kissed him. Her lips were hot and sweet, and pressed insistently against his. Then her tongue slid between his lips and she moaned. More than anything else it was the sound that excited him.

"I can't wait until tonight," she said, against his mouth. "I want you now."

"Now?" he said, looking around. "Here? Someone will come in, or see through the window."

"Come with me," she said, grabbing his hands and pulling him along, "come . . ."

She pulled him across the floor, away from the kitchen and through another doorway. She had both of his hands in hers, holding him so tightly he would have had to exert a lot of pressure to get free. If someone were to walk in at that moment with bad intentions he'd have a hell of a time getting his gun out.

As she pulled him through the doorway into the other room it occurred to him that it might be some sort of trap. However, once they got inside he saw that it was a storage room, and it was empty except for the two of them.

"Now," she said, releasing his hands and backing away from him, "nobody will see us in here."

He looked around. She was right. There were no windows, and even if someone entered the café they wouldn't be seen.

"Kitty," he said, "I really have to . . ."

He stopped when she peeled her dress down to her waist. She stood there for a moment with her hands on her hips, because she knew she was beautiful. Her breasts were big, but less pear-shaped than her sister's. She had the same pale skin and big pink nipples, but distended, they were even larger than Kate's had been.

She walked toward him, wrapped her fingers in his hair and pulled his face down to her. She kissed him fiercely, so hard that he knew his lips would probably be bruised. He was unable to resist her mouth, though, and her body as it molded itself to him. He put his arms around her then and kissed her back and the room filled with the sound of their breathing and the scent of sex.

He slid his hand down inside her dress, pushing it down so that it fell to her ankles. She had flimsy white underwear on and he slid his hand inside so that he could slide his middle finger along her moist cleft. She moaned and slid her hand down the front of his pants, feeling his huge erection.

He broke the kiss first and they both panted, out of breath. Her lips were puffy and her eyes glazed. He still had his hand inside her underpants and he allowed his finger to dip into her. She reacted with a start and a sharp "Oh!" and bit her lip.

Suddenly, he grabbed the flimsy garment and simply tore it from her. He then took her bottom in his hands and lifted her. He walked with her and set her on top of a crate, then knelt down and began to ravage her with his mouth. She gasped and cried out, grabbed his head and held it tight, as if she was afraid he might try to get away.

He wasn't going anywhere, though. He lifted her legs and put them over his shoulders so he could spread her open and then began to lick the length of her over and over again. He slid one finger inside her and worked his tongue over her until she couldn't stay still.

"God, oh God . . ." she gasped, and then instead of trying to hold him there she was trying to push him away. "Wait, wait," she gasped, "wait . . . I feel . . . I feel . . . like I'm gonna . . . gonna . . . die!"

But she didn't die. She went crazy as waves of pleasure washed over her. Her butt began to buck but he slid his hands beneath her again to hold her there while he delved into her with his tongue, relishing the taste of her, and the wetness of her all over his face . . .

He stood up, then, and hurriedly undid his pants, letting them fall around his ankles. He couldn't kick them away because he still had his boots on, and he had to set his gun belt aside but in that moment all he wanted was to be inside of her.

She scooted toward him and he entered her in one swift movement. She cried out and wrapped her legs and arms around him and he began to take her that way, her face buried in his neck, her breasts pressed against his chest, his hands cupping her round bottom and pulling her to him with every thrust of his hips.

"God, oh God . . ." she kept yelling, which was okay with him, because as long as she was yelling he knew she hadn't died . . .

TWENTY-SIX

"Oh, God," she said, again.

"What?" He paused in the act of pulling his pants back up.

She reached beneath herself and said, "I think I got a splinter in my, uh . . ."

"Oh, I'm sorry," he said. "That must have happened when I threw you up on the crate."

"Or when my butt was rubbing back and forth," she said.

"Well, let me see," he said. "Maybe I can get it out."

"Oh, no," she said, looking embarrassed, "I couldn't . . ."

"Kitty," he said, "you're naked, and after what we just did I don't think you should be embarrassed, do you?"

Now she looked sheepish and said, "No, I suppose not."

"Let me have a look."

"All right."

She got up on the crate on her hands and knees,

turned around and presented him with her butt.

"Oh, my . . ." he said.

"Is it a big splinter?" she asked.

"Oh, no," he said, "I just . . . you have a beautiful bottom . . ."

It was perfectly shaped and right in the center of the right cheek there was indeed a small splinter.

"I see it," he said.

"Can you get it out?"

"I'll try."

He leaned in close to take a look and the scent of her once again filled his nostrils. She smelled deliciously like a woman who had just had sex.

He touched the splinter and she jumped and said, "Ouch."

"I'm sorry."

"That's all right. Just get it out. I can't go all day with a splinter in my ass, can I?"

"No," he said, "you sure can't."

He leaned in close and, using his nails, was able to grab the very end of the splinter and pull it out.

"See," he said, holding it so she could see it, "I got it."

"It's funny how that small thing could hurt so much," she said.

"Well, that's how splinters are."

He dropped the splinter and stepped back.

"I think now that you got it out," she said, "you should kiss it and make it better."

She didn't have to ask that twice.

"My pleasure," he said.

He leaned forward and kissed her ass where the

splinter had been, then kissed it again, gently, and then
again.

"Is that better?" he asked.

"Mmm," she said, wriggling her butt, "more."

He put a hand on each side of her butt and kissed
each cheek lovingly, then slid his tongue along the cleft
between the cheeks. While he was doing that he slid
one hand between her thighs so that he could stroke
her. She was already wet so his fingers dipped right
into her and she sighed and moaned.

"Oh, God, now it feels better," she said.

"You think that feels better?" he said.

He took hold of both her cheeks, spread them and
then went to work with his tongue again . . .

"Where did you *learn* all that?" she asked just a little
later. She was out of breath, and there were butterflies
in her stomach. Also, her legs felt completely drained.
"I don't think I can stand."

She turned around on the crate again and sat gin-
gerly, so she wouldn't get another splinter. In this position he was looking right at her big, round breasts.
Her nipples were still hard so he leaned forward and
started to suck and bite them.

"God," she groaned, "why did you put your pants
back on?"

As her hands attacked his belt he was wondering that
very same thing himself.

Now his bare butt was banging against the crate. He
wasn't sitting on it, but he was leaning back against it
while she knelt between his knees, sliding his penis in

and out of her mouth, fondling his testicles, running her hands up and down his inner thighs, touching the little red marks where she had already bitten him.

He had his hands on her head and his legs slightly bent as she continued to suck him until he couldn't take anymore. He felt the build-up in his loins, like a molten river that ran up his legs and into his groin and then came bursting out and into her mouth. She slid her hands behind him then, to cup his buttocks and pull him toward her as he filled her mouth. She continued to suck him and moan until he had no more to give her and it became almost painful—but amazingly so.

"Mmm," she said, releasing him from her mouth and kissing his belly and his thighs, and then turning him so she could kiss his butt as he had kissed hers.

"I don't have a splinter," he said thickly.

"Mmmm," she said, with her mouth pressed to his butt, "I know . . ."

TWENTY-SEVEN

When Clint and Kitty came back out into the café Clint was surprised no one was there. It seemed to him they had been in the storeroom forever.

"Now what was it you wanted when you came here?" she asked.

"Uh . . . oh, I was looking for your sister."

"Maybe she came back."

Kitty ducked into the kitchen, and then came back out.

"She's not here. I don't know where she could be."

"Maybe she's still at the hotel," Clint said. "I'll check there."

"Okay," she said, touching his arm, "but if you don't find her there, come on back. We won't be busy for a while yet."

"Kitty . . ."

"I have to clean up in the kitchen," she said. "See you later."

Kitty went back into the kitchen and Clint went outside, stopping just outside the door. He couldn't believe what had just happened. He had been totally caught up in Kitty's body and had forgotten about everyone and everything else for that time.

He heard horses and looked up the street. He saw Bat and Luke Short riding into town, hell-bent for leather. They were in a hurry for some reason. He stepped out to greet them.

Kate rolled over in the bed, putting her back to the man. The man looked at her back, her butt, her smooth skin and still tasted her on his mouth.

"I don't believe you, Kate."

"What?"

"You hate me, right?"

"Right."

"Wish I was dead?"

"Yes."

"And yet you go to bed with me to keep me away from your sister," he said. "Is that right?"

"That's right."

"Well," he said, rolling onto his back, "you were good, real good . . . but it ain't gonna work."

She sat up abruptly and looked at him over her shoulder.

"What?"

"I'm still going after your sister."

"But . . . why?"

"Because she's the one I want."

"You bastard!"

"I never said I wouldn't go after her if you went to bed with me," he told her. "I said I'd consider it."

Kate got up, grabbed her dress and pulled it on

quickly. Suddenly, she felt as if she needed a bath—a scalding-hot bath.

"You sonofabitch—"

"Don't forget the tray outside the door," he said.

She glared at him with hatred in her eyes, then turned and stormed out of the room, slamming the door behind her.

Quite a woman, he thought, but unfortunately, not the one he wanted.

"What's chasing you guys?" Clint asked, as Bat and Short reined in their horses.

"We, uh, suddenly realized that we left you here alone," Bat said.

"Yeah," Short said, "we thought you might get yourself into some kind of trouble."

Clint thought about what he'd just been doing in the storeroom with Kitty and said, "No, no trouble. No trouble at all."

TWENTY-EIGHT

Clint decided to try to find Kate later. While Bat and Short took their horses back to the livery he went over to the saloon and got three beers. Caleb Cahill did not greet him in a friendly manner, and this time there were other men in the saloon drinking, so the man had an excuse to serve him and then ignore him, which suited Clint just fine.

By the time he got the three beers to a corner table Bat and Short walked in and joined him. The other men in the place knew who all three of them were, so they were the center of attention. None of them paid it any kind.

"So you didn't find anything out there?" Clint asked.

"Did you expect us to?" Bat asked.

"No."

"Well," Short said, "neither did we, but it was something to do."

"No likely hiding places, eh?"

"Not that we could see," Bat said. "What happened here?"

Clint told them about the Man on the Gray Horse.

"So you're convinced he's involved," Bat said.

"Yep."

"And that he's at the hotel?" Short asked.

"Right again."

"And that he's involved with the Cahills?" Bat asked.

"Well," Clint said, "I'm sure they know him, but not sure what the relationship is."

"So why don't we just go over to the hotel and find out what's going on?" Bat asked.

"Let's just wait a minute and think about this," Clint said.

"What's to think about?"

"He hasn't contacted us yet. What does that tell you?"

Bat and Short exchanged a glance, and then Bat said, "That he's still waiting for someone else."

"That's what I think," Clint said.

"Yeah," Short said, "but is he waiting on someone for his side, or our side?"

"I think he's waiting for another one of us," Clint said.

"And then what?" Bat asked. "Is he going to face us alone?"

"I guess that's something we'll have to wait and see," Clint said.

"Unless we go over there right now and ask him," Short said.

"No, Luke," Bat said, "I'll go along with Clint on this one. I think we should wait and see who we're waiting for. It might be interesting."

"Well," Short said, "nobody's tried to kill us yet, so I suppose there's no harm in waiting."

"Another day?" Bat asked.

Now all three of them exchanged glances, then held up their beer mugs.

"Another day," Clint said.

When Kate came out of the hotel she headed right for the café, but stopped short when she saw Clint Adams in front. She watched from a doorway, the food tray tucked under her arm, while Bat Masterson and Luke Short rode up to him and they all had a conversation. After that the two mounted men rode toward the livery, and Clint walked away from the café, probably heading for the saloon.

Once the coast was clear she came out of her doorway and hurried into the café.

"Where have you been?" Kitty asked.

"Don't ask," Kate said.

"You look all messed up!" Kitty said.

"So do you," Kate sad, "What happened here while I was gone? I saw Clint outside."

Kitty smiled.

"Kitty, you didn't," Kate said.

"Yes, we did."

"In here?"

"In the back."

"Someone could have caught you."

"Nobody did."

"How did it happen?"

"He came here lookin' for you," she said, "but he ended up staying because of me."

Kate frowned. It was irresponsible for her sister to have had sex in the café while the door was open, but then again maybe it kept Clint from coming over to the hotel looking for her.

"What did you do?" Kitty asked.

"It's not what I did," Kate said, "it's what I'm going to do."

"And what's that?"

"Take a bath," Kate said. "A hot one!"

TWENTY-NINE

Clint, Bat and Luke Short left the saloon after dark and walked over to the hotel together.

"One more day like this one," Short said, "and I'm gonna turn into a drunk."

"Whataya mean, turn into one?" Bat asked, and the other two men laughed.

Clint said, "I'm glad one of us can see straight enough to get us back to the hotel."

"That's right," Short said, "you didn't drink that much. How come?"

"I figured the two of you were drinking enough for all of us," Clint said.

"Oh, we're not that drunk," Bat said. "We're just kidding around."

"I know that."

"No, he's telling the truth," Short said. "We're not that drunk."

"I said, I know," Clint replied.

Short looked at Bat and said, "Is he humoring us?"

"Probably."

Clint knew his friends were not falling-down drunk, but they were impaired to a degree. Now would have been a fine time for somebody to open fire on the three of them, but they made it to the hotel without incident. As they entered the lobby Adam Cahill looked up from his desk.

"Can you two get up to your rooms alone?" Clint asked.

"We told you . . ." Bat said.

"We're not drunk," Short finished.

"Well then, up you go," Clint said.

"What are you going to do?" Bat asked.

"I'm just going to have a talk with our friendly desk clerk, here," Clint said.

"Well, don't go back outside without us," Bat said. "We got to watch each other's backs."

"I'm not going anywhere, Bat."

Together, the two men went up the stairs and managed to get to the top without falling back down again.

Clint approached the front desk, which seemed to make Adam Cahill nervous.

"What's the matter, Adam?"

"Hmm? Oh, nothin'."

"Something's on your mind."

"I don't know what you mean."

"Sure you do."

Adam tried to stare Clint down but could not. He averted his eyes and said, "I don't understand—"

"You've got a friend staying in your room, Adam," Clint said, and saw the surprise in the other man's eyes.

"I don't—"

"Don't bother denying it," Clint said. "I saw you talking to him."

"You saw . . . him?"

"No, I saw you," Clint said, "I didn't see him, but I saw you talking to someone in that room. Now, I don't care who he is, I just want you to tell him that whatever he's got in mind he better get on with it quick. We're not going to wait around here forever. Understand?"

"I don't—"

"Do you understand what I said?"

"Well, yes, but—"

"Then pass it on," Clint said. "That's all I'm saying."

Clint turned and left the desk. Adam Cahill stood there with his mouth open, waiting for Clint to go upstairs. When he was alone he turned and hurried down the hall.

"Again, Adam," the man said, "slowly tell me what he said."

Adam Cahill went through it again, telling the man everything Clint had said, word for word.

"All right," the man said.

"What are you gonna do?"

"Nothing, yet," the man said.

"But . . . he knows."

"He knows nothing," the man said. "He knows just what I expected him to know. I'm not going to let him force me to move before I'm ready."

"But we've got to—"

The man reached out and put his hand on Adam's shoulder, turned him around and opened the door.

"You did good, Adam," the man said. "Just keep

cooperating and your family is going to be very happy
they all met me."

He put his hand against the small of Adam's back
and pushed him gently out into the hall.

"Just don't let him or either of the others spook you,
Adam," he said, as a final word. "We'll move at my
pace."

"But—"

The man closed the door in his face, leaving Adam
standing out in the hall. He felt foolish, like a small
boy who had been given his instructions for chores,
and he didn't like the feeling. After all, he was the
head of the Cahill family.

He had to remember that.

Inside the room the man was rubbing his hands together. As he had expected Clint Adams was the one
figuring things out, but what a surprise it would be for
him when he discovered there was nothing to figure
out. He knew that Clint Adams, Bat Masterson and
Luke Short were expecting some big revelation to take
place. Well, that wasn't going to happen, and maybe
that would throw them off their stride long enough for
him to get his way.

First, though, he had to get to Kitty, and he'd have
to do that in the morning, because by the time the sun
went down tomorrow it was all going to be over.

The next morning he decided to take a big chance. He
grabbed his hat and strapped on his gun belt, left the
room and took the hall to the back door. He slipped
out that way so no one would see him, then used the

back alley to make his way to the street the café was on. If he happened to run into Clint Adams, or either of the other two, it really wouldn't matter. He thought that their curiosity would keep them from doing anything rash. The one he was going to have to worry about was Kate. She was real protective of her younger sister, and after what he'd pulled, forcing her to sleep with him, she was liable to do anything.

It really was too bad his preference ran to Kitty.

THIRTY

Kate looked up as Kitty came rushing into the kitchen.

"What is it?" she asked.

"Guess who just came in!"

"Who?"

"Take a look."

Kate went and looked into the dining room, a bad feeling in the pit of her stomach. She saw exactly who she didn't want to see.

"Stay away from him, Kitty," she said.

"Why? He's nice."

"He's nice to you," Kate said. "He hasn't been so nice to me, or to your brothers."

"What are you talkin' about?"

"I'm saying he's a bad man."

"A bad man?" Kitty asked. "You mean like Poppa and Uncle were bad men?"

"I'm saying he's bad for you—"

"Ain't that my decision?" Kitty asked. "Besides, right now all he wants is something to eat."

"He had something to eat."

125

"What? Where—"

"That's who I took the tray over to at the hotel."

"Why didn't you say so?"

Kate took her sister by the shoulders.

"Because I want you to stay away from him," she said. "He's forced Adam out of his room, and he's forced his way into our lives."

Kitty shook her head, then shook off Kate's hands.

"I don't understand," she said. "What's going on between him and Adam? Between him and you?"

"That's the trouble," Kate said. "I don't know what's going on between him and Adam. Our dear brother won't tell me."

"And you and him?"

Kate didn't answer.

"Do you want him for yourself?"

"God, no!" Kate said.

"But you been with him?"

After a moment Kate said, "Yes."

"So he's bad for me, but not for you?" Kitty asked. "Is that what you're saying?"

"No, that's not what I'm saying—"

"He wants steak and eggs," Kitty said. "Are you gonna make it for him, or am I?"

Kate took a deep breath.

"I'll make it."

"I'll bring him some coffee."

"Kitty—"

"I'm only waitin' on him, Kate," Kitty said. She grabbed a pot of coffee and a cup and walked out.

•   •   •

The man sat back as Kitty poured his coffee, and breathed in her scent. He wanted her so bad he could taste her, and having had her sister only whetted his appetite for her.

"Your food will be out in a minute," she said, and turned to leave.

He grabbed her wrist, firmly but not hard enough to hurt her. Only enough to delay her.

"What's the hurry?"

"I got work—"

"What did Kate tell you about me?"

Kitty stopped trying to turn away and looked at him.

"Nothin'," she said, "she didn't—"

"Oh yes, she did," he said. "You know, Kitty, I've got real strong feelings for you."

"You do?"

He nodded.

"I've talked to your brother Adam about me and you," he said. "I'd like to come courting."

"Oh . . ." she said, putting one hand to her throat.

"Now, Adam, he's not so dead-set against it," he said, "but your sister is. Why do you suppose that is?"

"She thinks . . . you're bad," Kitty said.

"Bad? Me?" He smiled, a wide, charming smile. "Do you think I'm bad, Kitty?"

"Well . . . I don't know . . ."

"You know what I think?"

"W-what?"

"I think Kate wants me for herself," he said. "Did she tell you she came to my room yesterday?"

"Yes."

"She tell you why?"

"To bring you some food."

"That was her excuse," he said. "As soon as she was in my room she took off her clothes, and I'm just a man, Kitty. I was weak, but I don't want Kate. I want you. I don't think she likes that."

Kitty was confused.

"After all," he said, "she's the older sister. How would it look if you got married first?"

"Married?" she asked, her eyes wide.

"That's what I'm talking about," he said. "Getting married, taking you away from here, settling down someplace. Would you like that?"

"Well . . ." she said, "I'd like to get married . . . someday . . . and I'd sure like to get away from here."

He released her wrist and said, "You think it over, Kitty. After all, the only decision that matters is yours."

"I— Uh, what are you askin' me, exactly?" she asked.

"I'm asking if you'll marry me."

"Oh," she said, again, this time putting both hands to her bosom. "Nobody ever asked me that before." She knew Rupert wanted to marry her, but he was her cousin and, besides, he hadn't actually come out and asked her.

"Well, I'm asking," he said, "but I'm not going to press you for an answer. You think it over, talk it over with Adam, or with Kate, if you want."

"A-all right—"

"And for now," he said, "I'll just have that steak and eggs."

"I'll go and get it," she said, and hurried off.

He watched her disappear into the kitchen, then saw the three men walk through the front door and forgot all about Kitty.

THIRTY-ONE

Clint, Bat and Luke Short met in the lobby that morning to walk over to the café together.

"This has been a waste of time," Short said as they walked.

"Sure as hell not worth a thousand dollars," Bat said.

"And our curiosity hasn't been satisfied at all," Clint said.

"Even one more night here seems silly," Bat said. He was surprised—as Clint was—that the Cahill sisters had not returned last night. Of course, it was possible that one—or both—of them had gone to Luke Short's room, but somehow neither Bat nor Clint thought that was true.

"You fellas were much quieter last night," Short said then, confirming both their suspicions. "I was able to sleep. I appreciate it."

"That's because I was alone," Clint said.

"So was I," Bat said.

"Oops," Short said. "Sorry. Did you fellas offend those nice girls the other night?"

"I don't think so," Bat said.

"Me, neither," Clint said, and he certainly hadn't done anything to offend Kitty yesterday in the storeroom, either.

When they reached the café they entered together. It was early and there was only one diner there ahead of them. Kitty was talking to him as they entered and then she rushed into the kitchen. The three of them went to the same table they'd used before. The other man was sitting on the other side of the room, and there was something familiar about him to Clint.

"Boys," he said, "I think our lives are about to get more interesting."

"He what?" Kate demanded.

"He asked me to marry him."

"That's crazy," Kate said. "He's only been here a few times before. You hardly know him."

"I know I want to get out of this town," Kitty said.

"We all do, Kitty."

"Well," Kitty said, "maybe you're just jealous that now I have a chance. Maybe you want him to ask you so you can have a chance."

"Ask me?" Kate said, eyes widening. "What the hell did he tell you?"

"He said you came to his room and . . ."

"He said *I* took *him* to bed, didn't he?"

"Well," Kitty said, "how could he force you? You ain't sayin' he raped you, are you?"

"No," Kate said. "He didn't rape me—not forcibly, anyway."

"Then what?"

Kate took a deep breath and let it out in a rush.

"He said he'd stay away from you if I slept with him."

"And you did?"

"Yes."

"And then?"

"And then he said he lied. I could have killed him then. If I'd had a gun or a knife I would have."

"He said it was you . . ."

"Well," Kate asked, "who are you going to believe, him or your own sister?"

Kitty picked up the plate of steak and eggs and said, "I don't know." She went out to bring the man his breakfast.

"You're saying that's him?" Luke Short asked.

"I think so," Clint said.

"Now that you mention it," Bat said, "it looks like him."

"We didn't see his face that clearly," Short said.

"Who else could it be?" Clint asked. "How many other riders came into town?"

"We don't know everybody who lives here," Bat said, "and in the area, but I'll agree it looks like him."

"I thought you said he was hiding out in the hotel?" Luke Short said.

"He was."

"Then what's he doing here?"

"Maybe today's the day he's going to make his move," Clint said.

"Against the three of us?" Bat asked. "What is he, suicidal?"

"Okay, then," Clint said, "he's going to make his pitch."

"Well then, I wish he'd make it," Short said. "I'm tired of waiting, and you guys have been here longer than I have."

"Well," Clint said, "maybe we should just force the action, then."

As he said it Kitty came out of the kitchen carrying a plate of food for the man, who smiled at her as she set it down. She hesitated, then came over to the three men.

"What can I get for you boys today?"

"What you brought that fella looks good enough to me," Clint said.

"Steak and eggs all around?"

"Sure," Bat said.

"Fine," Short said.

"Does he eat here often?" Clint asked.

"Him?" Kitty said. "No, he doesn't. He hasn't been here in a while."

"But he has been here before?"

"Yes," she said, "a time or two. I'll get your orders in." She turned and walked toward the kitchen.

"I guess you're right about one thing, then," Bat said.

"What's that?"

"There's some kind of connection to the Cahills."

THIRTY-TWO

The man watched Clint Adams, Bat Masterson and Luke Short eat and knew they were thinking about him. This pleased him. Let them wonder, he thought, and if they wanted to know let them come over and ask him. He was feeling good, in control and he wasn't afraid to take a chance. Maybe he'd even walk over there and . . . no, that wouldn't be taking a chance. That would just be foolishness, and things had gone too well for too long for him to start being foolish.

"So we're agreed?" Clint asked. "We'll all walk over there and join him?"

"If that doesn't rattle him," Bat said, "nothing will."

"If it doesn't rattle him," Short said, "we'll have gained a lot of insight into the kind of man he is."

"Yeah," Bat said, "crazy."

"Let's go."

They all stood up and, carrying cups of coffee with them, walked over to the table where the man was sitting alone.

• • •

There were still no other diners in the café and as the
three legendary gamblers and gunmen walked to his
table he instinctively knew they only wanted to talk to
him, to see if they could shake him up.

He stared up at them as they reached his table, and
they all sat down with him without speaking.

"Gents," he said, "can I help you?"

"We just thought we'd come over and join you," Bat
said.

"You looked lonely," Short said.

"I assure you I'm not," the man said, "but I am always willing to meet new people. You are . . . ?"

"You know who we are," Clint said.

"You sent us each a thousand dollars," Bat said.

"And an invitation to come here."

The man laughed and looked down at himself.

"Do these look like the clothes of a man who could
afford to give away three thousand dollars?"

"Maybe more," Bat said.

"We don't know exactly how many people you've
invited," Short said.

"So tell me, then," the man said, "am I in the habit
of giving away this much money?"

"We don't know," Bat said.

"We don't know what your habits are," Short said,
"but we would like to know why you asked us here?"

"Let me get this straight," the man said. "You had
no idea who invited you all here, and yet you came?"

"Curiosity," Bat said.

"It's a terrible disease," Short said.

The man looked at Clint, who had said very little up to this point.

"You just sit back and watch?" the man asked him. "While they do the interrogating?"

"One of us has to watch," Clint said.

"And what are you seeing?"

"A very calm man," Clint said, "who is not going to tell us a thing until he's ready."

"Well," the man said, "I am calm, but I'm afraid I don't have anything to tell you fellas at the moment . . . but if you give me some time I'm sure I can come up with something."

"You've got time," Clint said, sliding his chair back and standing up. Now it was Bat and Luke Short who were watching the other man. "You've got the rest of today, because tomorrow morning we're pulling out."

"What a shame," the man said, as Bat and Short also stood. "You're leaving and we've only just met."

"Have we?" Clint asked.

"Sorry?"

"We've never met before?" Clint asked. "Is that what you're telling me?"

"I think I'd remember three such gentlemen as you," the man said.

"I don't remember you at all," Clint said, "but you do look . . . familiar to me."

Now the man shifted uncomfortably.

"It's as if . . . I knew someone who looked like you."

"Is that so?"

"Yes," Clint said.

"You mean . . . like a brother?" Bat asked.

"Maybe."

"Or a father?" Short said.

"Could be."

The seated man now struggled to keep from revealing anything with his face or his demeanor.

"It'll come to me, though," Clint said.

"If we stay long enough," Bat said.

"Oh, right," Clint said. "That's right. If we stay long enough."

"Well, I have to thank you gents," the man said. "You've made my breakfast very interesting."

"We have one more day," Clint said to him, "to try to make your life interesting, as well."

The three of them walked away, never quite turning their backs on the other man.

THIRTY-THREE

"Well," Bat said outside the café, "what did that accomplish?"

"Like Luke said," Clint replied. "He didn't rattle, not until right at the end."

"That stuff about a brother or father," Short said. "Sometime, somewhere, we came in contact with his brother or father, and he's out for revenge."

"But what did we do?"

"It could be anything," Clint said. "It could be his father lost heavily in a poker game and was ruined, or killed himself."

"Not our fault," Bat said.

"What if the father complained he'd been cheated?" Clint asked. "And all these years he's been thinking about it."

"Still not our fault," Bat said, "but I get your point."

"Maybe," Short said, "we're not waiting for anybody else to show up."

"He can't be planning to handle us himself," Clint said. "Maybe we're not waiting, but he is."

"Remember," Bat said, "he's got the Cahills here—lots of Cahills."

"That's a good point," Clint said. "A very good point."

"Kitty," Kate said, after Clint, Bat and Luke Short had left, "whatever you do, don't give him an answer now. Talk to Adam first."

"Why should I?"

"Adam loves you," Kate said, "and he's the head of the family. He won't lie to you about this man—not when it's something this important."

Kitty bit her lip, then said, "All right. I won't give him an answer."

"And you'll talk to Adam?"

"Yes, Kate, I'll talk to Adam."

"Good," Kate said, "that's all I ask."

Now all she had to do was make sure *she* talked to Adam first.

"If we can pin down the Cahills," Bat said, "find out who this fella is and what their connection is, maybe we can take them out of play."

They were standing in front of the hotel, trying to figure out their next move.

"So who talks to them?" Short asked.

"We all do," Clint said.

"What?" Short asked.

"I'll talk to Adam; Bat, you talk to Caleb, the bartender; and Luke, you take Harley, the liveryman."

"What about the sheriff?" Bat asked.

"He's a cousin," Clint said. "Let's concentrate on the brothers."

"Sounds like a plan to me," Bat said. "At least it gives us something to do."

"We'll split up and meet in the saloon in two hours," Clint said. "One of us should know something by then."

"Hopefully," Bat said.

Kate wanted to talk to Adam as soon as possible, but the café was starting to get busy. She was going to have to wait until later, but the good thing was that Kitty would also have to wait.

The very good thing was that the man had finally left after Kitty told him she'd think about his proposal. Kate was standing in the doorway of the kitchen as he left and he gave her a satisfied smirk on his way out that made her want to smack it off his face.

"Come on, Kate," Kitty said, from behind her. "We're gonna get busy in a few minutes. Gotta get those eggs going."

THIRTY-FOUR

Because the café got busy, Clint was able to get to Adam Cahill before Kate did. Adam wasn't aware yet, but he was going to be very much in demand that day.

As Clint walked in Adam looked up from the desk.

"Are you always behind that desk?" Clint asked.

"I own the place and run it. If I'm not here, nobody is."

"We need to talk."

"Are you checking out?"

"No," Clint said, "none of us are, and I don't think you really want us to, do you?"

"I don't know what you mean."

"At least, not until your friend gets what he came for."

"What friend?"

"You know," Clint said, "the fella staying in your room? The one who came to town on a gray horse?"

Adam looked away.

"Look, Adam," Clint said, "we just talked to him over at your sisters' café."

"He went there?" Adam was clearly surprised.

"Yes."

"He must have went out the back."

"Why would he do that? What's he got to hide from you?"

Adam bit his lip, then said, "I don't want him near my sister."

"Kate?"

Adam shook his head.

"Kitty. Kate can take care of herself."

"So he's got eyes for Kitty."

Adam didn't say anything.

"Adam," Clint said, "I need to know his name."

"I—I can't tell you that."

"Why are you helping him?" Clint asked. "Are you and he close friends?"

"No!" Adam said, almost spitting the word out.

"Then what is it?"

No answer.

"Does he have something on you?"

No reply.

"Does he have something you want?"

That struck a nerve, but Adam didn't say a word. He wasn't able to hide the twitch of a facial nerve, or the widening of his eyes.

"Wait a minute," Clint said. "I get it now."

"There's nothin' to get."

"He found it, didn't he?"

Adam didn't answer.

"He found the hidden money—or he says he did. In exchange for helping him, he'll give it to you. Is that it?"

"You better leave before he gets back."

"Are you afraid of him?"

"No."

"Maybe just a little, right?"

"He's . . . good with a gun."

"Well then, you should be afraid of him," Clint said. "But you shouldn't let him walk all over you and your family."

"It's just until—" Adam started, but then stopped.

"Until what?" Clint asked. "Until you help him get what he wants? And then you get what you want? It's a bargain, right?"

"Men make bargains all the time."

"Sure," Clint said, "when there's something to bargain with."

"Whataya mean?"

"There are two possibilities, Adam," Clint said. "First, he didn't really find the money."

Adam didn't answer.

"Okay, I'll keep going. He didn't find it, or he did, and he showed you something that proved it, something else that your father buried with the money."

Adam looked away.

"I'm pretty close, huh?"

Adam was stubborn.

"Okay, here's the other thing," Clint said. "He sent me, Bat Masterson and Luke Short a thousand dollars each to come here. Where do you think he got that money, Adam?"

"A thousand—" Adam started.

"That's a total of three thousand," Clint said. "How much money did your father hide, Adam? Because if it was three thousand . . . well then, it's gone. He spent it. And even if there was more than three thousand, he spent three . . . that we know of. What if he spent the rest of it, too?"

"He didn't."

"How do you know?"

"He—he wouldn't."

"Why not?" Clint asked. "Because you have a bargain?"

Adam stuck his chin out stubbornly.

"You think a man like him will stick to a bargain?" Clint asked. "Think again, Adam. He using you, and your family. What does he want you and your brothers and your cousins to do, back his play against us?"

Adam didn't reply, but his silence was not as absolute as it had once appeared.

"Tell me his name, Adam," Clint said. "That's all I want. We'll figure out the rest when we know his name."

"He—he said he knew you," Adam said. "The three of you."

"But we don't know him."

"He came a few months ago," Adam Cahill said. "He knew about the money, said he found it."

"What did he show you to prove it?"

"A leather saddlebag that belonged to my father."

"So then there really was buried money?" Clint asked. "It wasn't just a myth?"

"Even I started to think it was," Adam said, "but he found it, damn him. He found it."

"And he said he'd trade it for your help."

"He wanted to use us, and the town."

"His name, Adam," Clint said. "Tell me his name and I'll leave you alone."

Adam stared at Clint for a few moments, then said, "He said his name is Evans."

"And a first name?"

"Ben."

"Benjamin Evans?"

Adam nodded, mortified at having broken a confidence, no matter what the situation.

"Benjamin Evans . . . Junior? Or just Ben Evans?"

"Just Ben Evans," Adam said. "So do you know him? Who is he?"

Bewildered, Clint said, "I don't know, Adam. I never heard of him before in my life."

THIRTY-FIVE

"Benjamin Evans?" Bat asked.

"That's right," Clint said. "That's what Adam said."

"It doesn't ring a bell for me," Short said.

"Me, neither," Bat said. "How do we know Adam gave you the right name?"

"Or that this fella gave Adam his right name."

"We don't know either of those," Clint said. "But this is what we have right now."

They were sitting out in front of the hotel, comparing notes. Actually, there weren't very many notes to compare. Bat and Short had come up empty with Caleb and Harley Cahill, who either didn't know anything, or were very, very dumb.

"Or both," Bat said.

"This is what we have to go on," Clint said. "The name Evans."

"If there was a telegraph office in this one-horse town we could find out about the Evans name," Bat said.

"But there isn't, so we can't," Clint said. "Okay, so

149

whether or not this is the man's name, we know how he's getting the Cahills to go along with him on everything."

"By dangling their family fortune in front of them," Bat said.

"Money that he's probably already pissed away," Short said.

"Some of it on us," Clint said.

"Hell," Bat said, "I'd give it back."

"Me, too," Short said. "I don't need an extra thousand that bad."

"Let's save that for later," Clint said.

"Do you think you got through to Adam?" Bat asked. "Will he and his family still stand with this Evans?"

"I don't know."

"They may be dumb," Short said, "but there's a lot of them."

"I know that," Clint said. "Maybe if I talked to Kate she could talk some sense into her brothers."

"This doesn't seem like the kind of family where a woman would have a lot of influence," Bat said.

"It's worth a try," Clint said.

"Well, then," Luke Short said, "start tryin'."

"Wha—" Clint started, but then he saw what Short meant. Kate Cahill was walking toward the hotel right at that moment.

"Want us to stay around and help?" Bat asked.

"She might talk more freely if it's just me," Clint said. "Why don't you fellas—"

"Yeah, yeah, we know," Bat said. "Find something to do. Come on, Luke. Let's take a hint."

As they went into the hotel Clint heard Short ask, "That was a hint?"

Kate saw the three men sitting in front of the hotel, but as she got closer two of them stood up and went inside. That left only Clint Adams.

"Hello, Kate," Clint greeted.

"Good afternoon, Clint," she said.

"Can I talk to you for a moment?"

"What's goin' on?" she asked.

"I just need to talk."

"I, uh, really came over to talk to Adam."

"That's what I want to talk to you about," Clint said. "Adam . . . and Ben Evans."

Kate stared at Clint for a few moments, and then she asked, "Adam told you his name?"

"He told me Ben Evans was his name," Clint said. "Is it?"

"As far as we know," she said. "That's how he introduced himself when he first arrived."

"And do you know about the money?"

"My family's mythical treasure?" Kate asked. "I know about it."

"Does it exist?"

"I doubt it."

"But Evans has your brother convinced that it does."

"Adam wants to believe in that money, Clint," she said. "It's a way for him to get out of here."

"And the rest of the family, too?"

She nodded. "We all want to leave."

"Badly enough to believe Evans and let him use you?"

"Apparently."

"Kate . . . you need to talk some sense into Adam. I doubt that there's any money—and if there ever was, I doubt there's any left. He can't believe what Evans is telling him."

"Don't you think I've told him that already? He won't listen. I'm only a woman, and he's head of the family."

"What were you coming here to talk to him about?"

"Kitty."

"What about her?"

"That madman . . . Evans asked her to marry him."

"What?"

"Adam has to stop him," she said. "I don't care about the money, but Kitty can't marry that man."

"I agree."

"Then help me convince Adam?"

"Why would your brother ever listen to me?"

"You got him to tell you Evans's name, didn't you?"

"I guess I did."

"Will you come inside with me?"

"Sure," he said, "why not? It's worth a try."

THIRTY-SIX

Adam saw Clint coming back into the hotel, this time with Kate. He began to look around for an escape route.

"Just stay there, Adam," she said. "We have to talk."

"About what?" he asked. "And why are you with him?"

"Would you rather I come in with Ben Evans?" she demanded. "Do you know what he did?"

"What?"

"He proposed to Kitty."

"What?"

"You heard me."

Adam hesitated, then asked, "Did she accept?"

"Not yet," Kate said. "I convinced her to talk to you first."

"All right," he said. "I'll talk to her. Why did you bring *him* with you?"

Kate looked at Clint, then back at her brother.

"To try to talk some sense into you."

"You don't have to," her brother said. "I don't want her to marry him, either."

"Not just about Kitty," Kate said. "About this whole mad plan."

"Kate," Adam said, "that's family business—"

"But it involves Clint and his friends," she said. "He has a right to be here."

"Kate—"

"Adam, I know you're doing what you think is best for the family," she said, "but it has to stop."

"I'm the head of the family," Adam said. "You don't tell me what has to stop."

"Adam—"

"Kate!" Adam snapped. "I don't care if you have him with you or not"—he pointed at Clint, but didn't look at him—"I make the decisions for this family."

"Maybe I should talk to the others," she said. "Maybe we should put this to a vote."

"A vote?" Adam asked. "We ain't never put nothin' to a vote in this family. If you want to try, go ahead, but Harley and Caleb and the others will stand with me."

Kate kept her mouth shut, because she knew her brother was right. She turned and looked at Clint, who truly did feel out of place in this brother and sister discussion.

She looked back at her brother and said, "You won't let him marry Kitty, will you?"

"No, I won't, Kate."

Clint decided to add his two cents at this point.

"That probably means you'll have to stand up to him, Adam."

Adam gave Clint a hard look, then averted his eyes. "I'll take care of it."

"You better," Kate said, "because if you let that man ruin her life—"

"Do you really think she could be worse off than now?" Adam asked, interrupting her. "Living in this ghost town?"

"I'm just warning you," Kate said. "If she leaves with that man I'll never forgive you."

She turned then, storming past Clint and out the front door.

"She's a tough lady," Clint said.

"I have nothing to say to you."

"Adam," Clint said, "my friends and I are not just going to stand still while you and your friend Evans do whatever you're planning to do. We'll fight all of you if we have to."

"There are a lot of us," Adam said, ominously, "a lot."

Which, Clint thought, was probably why Evans had chosen to align himself with this family at this time, in this place. There was always strength in numbers.

"Well," he said, "we'll be waiting."

That sounded lame even in his own ears.

"Very good, Adam," Ben Evans said, stepping out from behind the curtain where he'd been standing, listening.

"Why did you ask my sister to marry you?"

"Because she's beautiful," Evans said. "It's part of my plan to come out of this with a beautiful woman at my side."

"Not my sister."

"And what are you going to do?" Evans asked. He walked around the desk so he could lean on it and face Adam. "Are you going to stand up to me, like Adams said?"

"You heard what he said," Adam replied. "He and his friends aren't just gonna stand by and let us take them."

"Don't worry," Evans said. "Like you pointed out, there are a lot of you. Just have all your brothers and cousins here tonight, and we'll take care of them."

"They are the Gunsmith, Bat Masterson and Luke Short," Adam said. "Not just any three men."

"Adam," Ben Evans said, straightening up, "if they were just any three men, I wouldn't be here, and none of this would be happening."

He went back around the desk and hesitated at the curtained doorway.

"Remember," he said. "Have them all here."

He went through the curtain and Adam put his elbows on the desk and his head in his hands.

THIRTY-SEVEN

Clint found Bat and Luke Short and told them about the conversation with Kate, and the one with Adam Cahill.

"So that's all this is about?" Bat asked. "This Evans wants to make a name for himself, and the Cahills are going to back his lay?"

"That may not be all it's about," Clint said. "There's the myth about the money, there's the fact that Evans is trying to walk off with Kitty Cahill—"

"Well, clearly, that's not going to happen," Luke Short commented.

"Why do you say that?" Clint asked.

"Because if Evans is going to go up against us he's not going to walk away," Short said. "Hell, he wouldn't walk away going against *one* of us, let alone all three."

"Remember," Clint said, "we don't know exactly how many Cahills there are."

"And why did he pick us?" Bat asked.

"We have reputations."

157

"So do a lot of other people," Bat said. "Why us? Three men who know each other?"

"If I brought any three men with your kind of reputations here," Clint said, "they'd probably know each other."

"You, of all people, are calling this a coincidence?"

"Like I said," Clint answered, "there's a lot going on here."

"Well," Bat said, "I say we stay where they can find us, out on the street. I'm not gonna hide from these yahoos."

"We could ride out of town," Clint said.

Bat and Short exchanged a glance, and then said, "Naw," together.

"If word got out that we ran from a fight," Short said, "all three of us . . ."

"We'd be getting a lot more challenges than we're getting right now," Bat finished.

"Okay, then," Clint said. "Let's get out of this hotel."

When they reached the lobby there was nobody behind the desk.

"Something's going on," Clint said.

"Why do you say that?" Bat asked.

"Because Adam Cahill never leaves the front desk," Clint said. "Boys, let's be on our toes from here on out."

As they went out the door Bat said, "I thought we *were* being on our toes."

•　　•　　•

The Cahill clan gathered in the livery stable. Adam was in the center of the Cahill circle. Forming the circle were his brothers, Harley and Caleb, his cousin Rupert—the sheriff—and about a dozen other Cahill first, second and distant cousins. They were all wearing guns, and some of them were carrying rifles.

"When does this Evans fella want us to go ahead?" Harley asked.

"He'll give the signal," Adam said. "We just have to be ready to move."

One of the distant cousins looked around, cleared his throat and asked, "You think we got enough men for these three fellers? I mean, considerin' who they are?"

"Evans is supposed to be real good with a gun," Adam said. "He'll probably take care of one of them himself, which'll leave the other two for us. I think we got enough guns."

There was some shifting of feet and muttering, but nobody raised any objections or made any more comments. One man, however, did ask another question.

"Is there gonna be enough money to go around?"

Somebody looked at him and said, "Since five dollars is a lot of money to you, Will, I reckon the answer's yes."

"Don't worry," Adam said. "There'll be enough. Okay. Stay in town, stay out of sight."

The Cahill clan started filing out of the livery, some out the back door and some out the front. When most were gone all that was left was Adam, Harley, Caleb and the sheriff, Rupert.

"We got another problem, boys," Adam said.

"What's that?" Caleb asked.

"Evans wants to take Kitty with him when he leaves."

"As a hostage?" Harley asked.

"No," Adam said, "as his wife."

"What?" Rupert exploded. "What the hell—you—you can't let him do that, Adam."

"I don't intend to, Rupert," Adam said. "But I ain't gonna say nothin' until we got the money. Everybody got that? Nobody does nothin' until we get our money."

"She can leave with him if she wants to, as far as I'm concerned," Caleb said, with a shrug.

"What?" Rupert said.

"Me, too," Harley said. "Ain't no skin off my nose."

"Whataya talkin' about?" Rupert demanded. "She's your sister, damn it."

"What are you so hot about?" Caleb asked. "She's *our* sister, not yours."

"Okay, that's it, boys," Adam said to his brothers. "Get back to work."

Harley and Caleb broke away, leaving Adam alone with Rupert.

"No, Rupert," Adam said, "ya gotta understand this. Don't do nothin' until we get our money."

"I ain't lettin' him take Kitty."

"I ain't, either," Adam said, "but we can't do nothin' until he gives us the money. Understand? Understand, Rupert?"

"I understand," Rupert muttered.

"Okay, then," Adam said, "go on back to your office."

Sheriff Rupert Cahill left the livery and headed back to his office. He was going to load his best rifle and keep it ready, because if Ben Evans tried to take Kitty away, there was a bullet marked for him, money or no money.

Adam Cahill was alone with his thoughts in the livery when his brother Harley came up behind him.

"Harley," he said, "I thought you were going back to work."

"This is where I work, Adam," Harley reminded him.

"Oh, right . . . tell me something, Harley."

"What's that?"

"If Kate came to you and wanted you to vote on something, a decision I made for the family—"

"You're the head of the family, Adam," Harley said, interrupting his older brother. "Why would we vote on anything?" He seemed genuinely confused by the question.

"Don't worry, Harley," Adam said. "We're not." He patted his brother on the shoulder and left the livery.

THIRTY-EIGHT

From their vantage point in front of the hotel, Clint, Bat and Luke Short saw several men walking through town from the direction of the livery. Eventually, they saw the sheriff walking their way, his head down, seemingly very occupied by something.

"Looks like a family meeting took place," Clint said.

Some of the men passed them by and did not give them a second look. They all had the big Cahill ears, making it obvious that they were part of the family.

"Wonder what it was about?" Luke Short asked.

"Yeah," Bat said, "that's a hard one."

As the sheriff passed within earshot Clint called out, "Big family meeting, Sheriff?"

Sheriff Cahill looked up and appeared surprised to see them there.

"Huh? Meeting about what?"

"That's what we were wondering."

The lawman shook his head, still looking preoccupied.

"I got a lot on my mind, Adams," he said, and walked off.

"He doesn't look happy," Bat said.

"I wonder what's on his mind?" Short asked.

"I think I might have an idea," Clint said.

"What?" Bat asked.

"Kitty."

"What about her?"

"Kate told me that the sheriff wanted to marry her."

"They're related," Short said, then added, "not that that's stopped a lot of people."

"That's right," Bat said. "If Rupert heard about Evans proposing to her he wouldn't be happy at all."

"Might be something we can use to our advantage," Clint said.

"You never know," Bat said, nodding.

Last, but not least, Adam Cahill came walking up to the hotel.

"Not like you to leave the hotel untended, Adam," Clint said, as Cahill approached the door.

"You might have lost some business," Bat said.

"I doubt it," Cahill said. "Who'd want to register here?"

"We did," Bat said.

"Not that we had much choice," Clint said.

"You got some complaints about the accommodations?" the hotel owner asked.

"Nope," Bat said.

"Best in town," Luke Short said.

"What was going on at the livery, Adam?" Clint asked. "Little family meeting? Maybe a family confrontation?"

"Just some family business," Cahill said. "No confrontations."

"Were Kitty and Kate included in the meeting?"

"Family meetings are just for men."

"Ah, I see," Clint said. "The women just have to go along with the decisions that are made, huh?"

"That's right," Adam Cahill said. "That's the way it's always been, and the way it always will be."

"Unless Kate gets her way, huh? And gets some of the family to vote?" Clint asked.

"That's not gonna happen."

"Well, that's good, then," Clint said, "because that means that when the wrong decision is made, it'll be all the fault of one person—you. And how many more decisions do you think they're going to let you make after this one goes wrong, Adam?"

"I got to go inside," Cahill said. "You gents stayin' another night?"

"We are."

"You best settle up, then."

"Now?"

"As good a time as ever," Cahill said, and went inside.

"He wants us to pay for our rooms now," Clint said.

"Guess he figures we might not be alive to do it later," Bat said.

"Wish we knew what went on at that meeting," Luke Short said.

"Maybe Kate will know," Clint said.

"She wasn't there, remember?" Bat asked.

"Well, if I know her—and I think I do, at this point—she'll get the results from one family member or another. Why don't you fellas take care of our bills and I'll go see what she knows?"

"We'll meet you there," Bat said. "I'm starting to get hungry."

"Yeah," Short said, as they all stood up. "If I'm going to die I want to do it on a full stomach."

THIRTY-NINE

"You're getting to be a regular here," Kitty said as Clint entered.

"I have to talk to Kate."

"She's in the kitchen," Kitty said. "I was on my way out."

"Where are you off to?"

"To talk to my brother Adam. See you."

She went out the front door. There were no diners in the place so Clint went to the kitchen and stuck his head in.

"I'm glad you're here," Kate said. "I wanted to apologize for before."

"What did you do that you have to apologize for?"

"I asked you to go in the hotel with me, and then I just stormed out of there without you."

"That's okay," he said. "You were upset. I just saw Kitty on her way out."

"Yes, she's gong to talk to Adam now about Evans."

"What do you think she's going to do?"

"I don't know," Kate said. "Maybe if you asked her

167

to leave with you she'd forget about him."

"Maybe she'll just leave with whoever was alive when this is all over."

She turned away from the stove and faced him.

"You and your friends should leave."

"Why is that? Worried about us?"

"To tell you the truth I'm worried about my family," Kate said. "They seem to have gotten caught in the middle of something."

"That's funny."

"What is?"

"I was thinking that my friends and I have gotten caught in the middle of something."

She frowned.

"Well, whoever's in the middle, a lot of people are going to get hurt, or killed, including my brothers and my cousins."

"That does seem likely," Clint said, "unless . . ."

"Unless what?"

"Well, apparently there was a big Cahill family meeting in the stable a little while ago," Clint said.

"I wouldn't know," she said. "We women don't get invited."

"Well, they came to some kind of a decision," Clint said.

"What decision could they have come to?" she asked. "They just all do whatever Adam tells them to do."

"Maybe," Clint said, "you could talk them out of it."

"I doubt it."

"Isn't it worth a try?" Clint asked. "Look, my friends and I aren't leaving, and neither is Ben Evans. That leaves you and your family. If your menfolk would not back Evans, he'd have no play."

"Do you really think that?"

"There's no way he'd go against the three of us alone."

She bit her lip.

"I guess I could talk to them," she said. "There'd be no harm in that."

"And another thing?"

"What?"

"Your cousin Rupert, he can't be too happy about Evans proposing to Kitty."

"I hadn't thought of that," she said. "Rupert is a hothead."

"You might have a talk with him."

"Good idea."

"Kate," Clint said, "we don't want to hurt anyone in your family."

"I appreciate that."

"But we won't just sit back and be taken."

"I know that."

"This should be between Evans and us."

"I agree."

"Do what you can to get your family out of it."

"I will."

"And do it quick," he said. "I think we're very close to having this powder-keg go off."

"All right," she said. "Maybe I'll just close up for the rest of the day and see what I can do."

"Where will people eat?"

"They'll have to stay home and make their own food."

"Good luck, then."

She smiled and said, "Thanks."

As he was leaving he was wondering where he and Bat and Luke Short were going to eat.

He was walking toward the hotel when he heard Kate call his name. He turned and she came running up to him.

"Here."

"What's this?"

She handed him a basket of food.

"I realized after you walked out that if I closed you and your friends would have nowhere to eat. There's some cold chicken and some biscuits in there."

"Thanks very much," he said. "Bat and Luke will appreciate it."

"And you?"

"Yes," he said, "me, too."

"I hope—" she said, and stopped.

"What?"

"I hope we can . . . keep from having something really bad happen, Clint," she said. "I mean . . . it would really be bad."

"Yes," he said, "it would be."

She nodded, then turned and ran back to the café.

FORTY

"It's almost time."

The voice came from behind Adam. He turned and saw Ben Evans standing in the curtained doorway. Suddenly, the man stepped back and closed the curtains. Adam turned and saw Kitty enter the lobby.

"Hello, Kitty."

"Adam, we have to talk."

"Yes," Adam said, aware of Evans's presence just behind the curtain, "we do."

"That man, Evans," she said, "he . . . he wants me to leave with him when he's finished here."

"And do you want to?"

"I want to leave here," she said. "I don't know him well—actually, I don't know him at all. Why would he want me?"

"Because you're beautiful?"

"Is that the only reason?"

"I don't know, Kitty," he said. "I don't know him well, either."

"What should I do?"

"You should do whatever you want to do."

"Kate doesn't want me to go with him, but—"

"But what?"

"I don't know . . . if she wants him for herself."

"Does she know him better than you do?"

"N-no."

"I don't think she's interested in him."

"I don't know what to do."

"Do you love him?"

"No," she said, "but I want to leave here."

"So leave," he said. "Do you need a man to do that?"

She bit her lip and said, "Yes. I wouldn't know what to do or where to go alone."

"Then maybe you should just stay here with your family, Kitty."

"You're the head of the family, Adam," she said. "Tell me what to do, and I'll do it."

There it was, the big question. If he told her not to go with him how would Evans react from behind the curtain? Would Evans kill him right away? No, because then the rest of the family wouldn't help him. Would he hold back the money? Did Adam want the money bad enough to give up his sister?

"I'll have to . . . think about it, Kitty," he said. "Can I do that?"

"All right."

"We'll talk again tomorrow."

"All right, Adam. Thanks."

Kitty turned and left. The curtains swished open behind him and Ben Evans stood there, glaring at him.

"What was that about?" the man demanded.

"It was about protecting my family's interest until we get what we've got comin' to us."

"I'm taking your sister with me when I go, Cahill."

"And I'll tell her to go," Adam said, "after we're finished with our business."

"Our business is going to end tonight, before dark. Clint Adams and the others think that I'm waiting for someone else to get to town. Either someone else who, like them, was invited, or else someone who will back my play—but nobody else is coming. We're all here, Adam, all of us who are going to take part in a little history today."

"What history?"

"No one has ever gunned down three men like Adams, Masterson and Short at one time. Today is going to be the day."

"Is that what this is all about?" Adam asked. "Makin' a name for yourself by killin' them?"

"What did you think it was about?"

"I thought you had some reason to want to kill 'em," Cahill said. "I thought you wanted revenge for somethin'."

"Yeah," Evans said, laughing, "I'm sure they're thinking the same thing. Adams even thinks he knows me from somewhere. Do you know where he knows me from?"

"No, I don't."

"His worst nightmares," Evans said, "but his nightmares are about to end. Is your family in position?"

"They're all in town, waitin'."

"Good. I'll be on the street in one hour, Adam, and

you and them better all be there, ready to back my play."

"We'll be there," Cahill said.

"I'm going to my room to prepare."

"Can I ask a question?"

"Go ahead."

"Why do you want to take them all at once?' Adam asked. "Why not one at a time, by yourself?"

"One at a time would take too long," Evans said. "I would've had to find one, make my play, and then find the next one. Once I got the idea of sending them the money and getting them here, everything fell into place."

"And the money?" Adam asked. "Where did you get that?"

"Well, you know where I got that, Adam," Evans said. "I stumbled over it, found it just lying in the ground. Ain't that the best way to come across money?"

"You spent our money?"

"You'll get your money back, Adam," Evans said. "Every penny, as soon as I get what I want."

"One hour," Adam said.

"One hour."

FORTY-ONE

Instead of just sitting in front of the hotel they decided to walk around town. With three sets of eyes they doubted that anyone would be able to try something on the street, plus they doubted that bushwhacking was going to be the way it was done.

They made one circuit of the town and headed back to the hotel. As they came within sight of it Clint said, "Hold on."

"What is it?" Bat asked.

"Look at what Adam is doing."

They all looked across the street and saw Adam Cahill closing the front door of the hotel from the outside, and locking it with a key.

"Step in here," Clint said, moving into a doorway. Bat and Short followed. It was a tight fit, but they made it.

"He locked the hotel up," Bat said.

"That door hasn't been locked the whole time we've been here, has it?" Short asked.

"No," Clint said. "He keeps the hotel open all the time."

"It's today," Bat said.

"It's now," Luke Short said.

"Maybe the next hour or so," Clint said.

"Well, now, an hour, whatever," Bat said, "it's going to be a relief to get this over with."

"We may not get any answers, though."

"What do you mean?" Bat asked.

"If it happens and we kill Evans, we'll never know why he brought us here," Clint said.

"Well," Short said, "there could be two reasons. One, he wants to make a name for himself and two, his revenge."

"I vote for the first one," Bat said. "He lured us here with the thousand dollars, got our curiosity up so he could kill all three of us at one time and make a huge name for himself."

"Well," Clint said, "I thought he looked familiar, but now I think I was just trying too hard. I agree with you, Bat. He got us here because we're too curious for our own good."

"And we have big egos," Bat said. "Don't forget that."

Clint looked at him.

"You brought it up first!" Bat said.

Clint looked at Short.

"Hey, you did."

"Fine," Clint said, "he got us here, and he's got the whole Cahill clan to back his play. They don't even have to be good with a gun, if they've got pure numbers on their side."

They stepped out of the doorway and looked around.

"What do you think?" Bat asked. "Rooftops?"

"It looks like a damned ghost town," Clint said, "but I'll bet they're everywhere, waiting for the word."

"You mean," Bat said, "behind every door and window?"

"And maybe even on the rooftops," Clint said.

"If they just open fire," Short said, "we're dead, boys."

"No," Clint said, "he won't do it that way. He's going to want to talk to us first, rub it in. Tell us how he outsmarted us."

"He'd do better just to have them open fire," Bat said.

"He's not that smart."

"Smart enough to get us here," Luke Short.

"Okay," Clint said, "for now let's stay off the street."

"Should we cross over to the hotel?" Bat asked. "Wait for it there?"

"This is as good a place as any," Clint said. "Let's keep the hotel in sight, in case that's where Evans comes from."

"He's going to have to use a back door to get out," Bat said.

"He'll still have to come up the alley," Clint said. "He's got to get to the street sometime."

"I wonder where the women are?" Bat said. "Kate and Kitty."

"Indoors, I hope."

"Yeah," Bat said, "I hope so, too."

• • •

They remained where they were, looking up and down the street, across the street, behind them, watching doors, windows and rooftops.

"We still have time to ride out," Luke Short said.

"You're the one who said he couldn't run from a fight," Bat said, checking his gun.

"I know," Short said, "I still feel that way."

"Then why make the comment—"

"I'm just making conversation," Short said.

Clint checked his own gun, then holstered it. His rifle was in his room, but the hotel was locked.

"Where are your rifles?" he asked.

"In my room," Short said.

"Mine, too," Bat said.

"Locked inside the hotel," Clint said. "We're some smart gunfighters, huh?"

"I'm not a gunfighter," Short said, "I'm a gambler."

"I'm not a gunfighter, either," Clint said.

"Then why make the comment?" Bat asked.

"I'm just making conversation."

FORTY-TWO

It was time.

Ben Evans left his room, walked down the hall to the rear of the hotel and went out the back door. His heart was pounding, but that was okay. He'd been planning for this day for a long time, most of his life. Maybe not this specific day with these specific men, but for a day like this when he would make a name for himself.

First he outsmarted them and got them here, and now he would outsmart them again and shoot them down. It didn't matter that he had the Cahills gathered and ready to do most of the shooting. When the word went out it would be his name they would talk about, and no one else's. The story would get around, and it would change with each telling, until the day it was told that he faced three men—three legends of the West—and he was the only one who walked away.

Now all he had to do was make it happen.

•   •   •

When Ben Evans came walking out of the alley all three spotted him at the same time.

"Here he comes," Clint said.

"I could shoot him now," Bat said. "Be all over."

Clint and Luke Short considered the suggestion, but then rejected it.

"Don't forget," Clint said, "this story is going to get told again and again. Let's make sure we come out of this looking good."

"Don't know how that's gonna happen," Bat said, "seein' as how we were dumb enough to get ourselves into this in the first place."

"I say right now we don't look so dumb," Luke Short said.

"Whataya mean, Luke?"

"Look up and down the street," Short said. "You see anyone else?"

They didn't see anyone. The street was completely empty.

"Maybe he hasn't given his signal yet," Clint said.

"Look at him," Bat said. "He's looking up and down the street, too."

"Let's go and talk to him," Clint said. "Maybe he's having a change of heart."

"Okay," Bat said, "but let's keep a sharp eye out, huh? These Cahills could still jump out of the wood-work at us."

"I'll cover the rear," Short said, and they stepped into the street.

As the three men crossed the street toward him Ben Evans looked up and down the street and on the rooftops, his mouth dry. The signal was supposed to be as soon as he appeared on the street. As soon as he walked out of that alley the Cahills were supposed to start appearing.

There was not a Cahill in sight.

Farther down the street Adam and Kate Cahill watched from a window. They had a good view, but could not be seen from the outside.

"Adam, thank you," Kate said, squeezing her brother's arm.

"You had half of them talked out of it anyway, Kate," Adam said.

"Rupert was the hard one," she said. "He wanted to kill Evans himself."

"How did you talk him out of it?"

"I didn't," Kate said. "Kitty did. She's, uh, keeping him busy."

Adam looked at his sister. "I thought you were against cousins doin' that sort of thing?"

"I figured it was the lesser of two evils. What finally made you change your mind, Adam? It wasn't me."

"I guess it was just time to stop believing in a myth."

"But you said you thought Evans actually did find the money."

"Some money, yes," Adam said. "But not a fortune, Kate. Ain't enough money in the ground to pay all these Cahills to back his play. For that he'd need a real fortune, and he ain't got it. And he'd need even more than that to buy my baby sister."

Kate squeezed her brother's arm again and said,

"Today you really have become the head of the family, Adam."

"I ain't no wiser or no richer," Adam said.

"As far as I'm concerned, you're both," Kate said.

Clint, Bat and Short stopped about twenty feet from Ben Evans, who was looking real disappointed, and real worried.

"Looks like you're on your own, Ben," Clint said. "Not quite the way you had it planned, is it?"

"Damned Cahills," Evans swore. "Damned inbred idiots."

"Looks to me like they just got smart," Bat said.

"They ain't getting any money, that's for sure," Evans said.

"What money was that, Ben?" Clint asked. "Did you even have any left after what you sent us?"

"No," Evans said.

"And did you even find that in the ground?"

"No," Evans said, "I saved it."

"Just for this day, huh?" Short asked.

"Looks like it wasn't money so well spent, huh, Evans?" Bat asked.

"I hope you don't expect us to give it back?" Clint asked.

Evan studied the three men, and he was not as un-rattled as he had been in the café.

"W-what are you gonna do?" he asked. "You can't just gun me down. Three against one, that ain't fair."

"Oh, and what were the odds you had in mind for us, Ben?" Clint asked. "Three against twenty?"

"Can you even use that gun?" Bat asked.

Evans looked down at the gun on his hip, as if he'd just noticed it was there.

"I can use it."

"Really?" Clint asked. "Well, I tell you what, Ben. Since you went through all the trouble to get us here, we'll let you try to take one of us. That way maybe you can still make a name for yourself. What do you say?"

"It ain't fair," Evans said. "If I win the other two will kill me."

"Nope," Clint said, "they won't. It'll be one against one in a fair fight. That's the way reputations are made, Ben. One on one. You've got our word."

"Whataya say?" Bat asked.

"You get to pick," Short said.

Evans looked from one to the other, licking his lips nervously.

"I, uh, can ride out of town," he said. "You'll never hear from me again."

"That's not one of the options, Ben," Clint said. "You see, you set this up, and there's got to be a resolution. Besides, I don't believe you. I think we would hear from you again, and I for one don't want to."

"Me, neither," Bat said.

"So make your choice," Short said.

"Either me," Clint said, "or Masterson."

"Hey," Luke Short said.

"You've got that dumb holster sewn into the inside of your jacket, Luke," Clint said. "That's not going to do it in this instance."

"I'll borrow one of your gun belts."

"Not mine," Clint said.

"Not mine, either," Masterson said.

"Well now," Short said, "that ain't fair."

There was no way to know whether or not Evans was actually good with a gun, and both Bat and Clint thought—knew—that they were better than Luke Short was. This was their way of protecting their friend.

"Let's go, Evans," Bat said.

"Pick, Ben."

"T-this ain't right," the man said, looking like he was going to run.

"If you start running," Bat said, "I'll shoot you in the ass first, and then the chest. Everybody will know you got shot in the ass while running away."

"All right, all right," Ben Evans said. "Masterson."

Bat looked at Clint and shrugged.

"Okay," Clint said. He and Short moved off to one side. Clint thought that if, by some miracle, Evans outdrew Bat he'd be hard-put not to kill the man on the spot, word or no word.

"So what do we do with the money when this is over?" Short asked Clint.

"I say we give it to the Cahills," Clint said. "It may not be the buried treasure they've always dreamed about, but it's something."

"Okay. Bat's money, too?"

"Why not ask him?"

"I mean, you know, just in case—"

"Shut up."

Evans licked his lips. His heart was hammering in his chest harder than ever—so hard he thought he'd die before he could draw his gun. What had he been thinking? How could he have gotten himself into this, all for a rep and a pretty woman. Goddamnit it, he thought, God-just-damnit!

And he drew.

Bat fired once, then walked over to the body and looked down. From down the street people began to appear, walking toward them, but none were carrying guns.

Clint and Short walked over and stood next to him, looking down at Ben Evans.

"He would have come back, you know," Short said. "We would have seen him again."

"I know," Bat said, holstering his gun. "Don't make it any easier." He looked at his two friends. "This could have been avoided, you know."

"I know," Clint said.

"I don't know what's wrong with us," Short said.

Clint shook his head and said, "We're getting dumber as we get older."

"Amen," Bat Masterson said.

Watch for

THE POSSE MEN

231st novel in the exciting GUNSMITH series
from Jove

Coming in March!